"Come on, Otto," Moe said. "It's just bananas.
Nothing to be scared of."

When she looked where he was pointing, she saw the biggest, hairiest spider she had ever seen.

The giant brown spider crept slowly toward them across the floorboards. It looked almost six inches wide—as big as Moe's outstretched hand. The creature paused as if to consider its surroundings. Moe watched, fascinated. But when she looked at Otto, she noticed that his face had changed to pale green.

"Don't worry, Otto," she said quietly. "I'm sure it won't hurt us." She tiptoed to the nearby bargain counter and grabbed a thirty-cent genuine pressed-glass berry dish. She crept across the floor, past quivering Otto, and circled slowly. The spider reared up on its back legs and made a threatening noise that sounded like a low purr. Moe clamped the berry dish upside-down over the spider.

Otto's knees buckled. He fell to the floor with a *clunk*.

Books by Laurie Lawlor

The Worm Club
How to Survive the Third Grade
Addie Across the Prairie
Addie's Long Summer
Addie's Dakota Winter
George on His Own
Heartland: Come Away with Me
Heartland: Take to the Sky

Heartland Series

Take to the Sky

Laurie Lawlor

Illustrated by Jane Kendall

A MINSTREL® BOOK

Published by POCKET BOOKS
New York   London   Toronto   Sydney   Tokyo   Singapore

This book is a work of fiction. Names, characters, places and incidents are products of the author's imagination or are used fictiously. Any resemblance to actual events or locales or persons, living or dead, is entirely coincidental.

A MINSTREL PAPERBACK *Original*

A Minstrel Book published by
POCKET BOOKS, a division of Simon & Schuster Inc.
1230 Avenue of the Americas, New York, NY 10020

ISBN: 0-671-53717-2

First Minstrel Books printing September 1996

10 9 8 7 6 5 4 3 2 1

A MINSTREL BOOK and colophon are registered trademarks of Simon & Schuster Inc.

Cover art by Diane Sivavec

Printed in the U.S.A.

For my sisters,
Julie, Kerry, and Marcy

Take to the Sky

Chapter 1

Moe watched, speechless. She stood at the edge of
the boisterous Independence Day crowd gathered
in Norman Dubie's baked, stubbled field and
waited. Was Art Taylor really going to skyjump
the way the posters in town had promised? Sweat
trickled down Moe's forehead and eyebrows. Her
scalp and bright red hair felt hot enough to burst
into flames. She kept her eyes welded to the five
strong men who struggled to hold the ropes secur-
ing the bucking silk balloon that was being inflated
with smoke and air from an oil fire burning in a
small cart.

Confident as an angel, Taylor slipped inside the
crudely woven compartment that hung beneath the
red hot-air balloon. This lightweight basket had an

opening at the top so that just Taylor's smiling face, chest, and hand holding the release rope could be seen. When he gave a thumbs-up signal, the men dropped the ropes. Slowly, silently, the balloon rose, and the crowd cheered.

The late-afternoon breeze lifted the balloon and capsule higher and higher over Luck, Wisconsin. Soon Moe could no longer see Taylor's face. She could no longer make out the words "Taylor Terrific" painted on the capsule. What if his balloon never stopped climbing? How would Art Taylor get home again?

Suddenly, Art Taylor leapt from the balloon's capsule and began falling. A woman screamed. Another covered her face with her hands. Moe held her breath. She could not take her eyes away. Faster and faster, his long dark shape plunged toward earth. At the last moment—a miracle. A parachute opened. White, fragile fabric fluttered and filled with air. And there was Art Taylor, safe and sound! He dangled from the parachute's rope harness, swinging and waving, carefree as a hero.

The crowd went wild. Dozens of men tossed their best flat straw hats into the air. They slapped one another on the back. Boys whistled, jumped, and punched each other with delight. Girls and women waved handkerchiefs and applauded. Some sobbed openly. Others stared skyward in a daze as the red balloon became smaller and smaller and finally disappeared.

It was at that moment, precisely three thirty-one in the afternoon on July 4, 1908, that eleven-year-old Moe made up her mind. One day she, too, would take to the sky.

"Look over there! He's coming down in Stabler's cornfield!" someone shouted. A group of boys whooped and ran to greet Taylor.

Moe couldn't move. Her knees felt weak, rubbery, she was so overcome by longing.

"Only birds belong in the sky," grumbled a farmer standing beside her. "Taylor coulda killed himself."

"That's right," his neighbor said, nodding. "If humans was meant to fly, they woulda been born with wings."

Later that summer, Moe discovered that there were indeed humans who knew how to fly. Their names were Wilbur and Orville Wright, two brothers from Ohio. The Milwaukee newspaper said they had designed and built a self-powered airplane. On August 8, 1908, Wilbur flew the airplane above a race course in a faraway place called Le Mans, France.

When Moe showed the front-page story to Mother, she declared the whole thing a hoax.

"I believe in progress, my dear," Mother said, "but I don't believe that people will ever fly."

"But it says so right here in the newspaper," Moe insisted. " 'In a flash the catapult had acted. Mr. Wright was shot into the air while the spectators gasped in astonishment.' Three thousand French people saw him fly forty miles per hour."

"What do French people know?" Mother said, and sniffed. "Forty miles an hour! Who ever heard of anyone going that fast?"

Moe rolled her eyes. "But someone took a picture of Wilbur Wright flying in a perfect circle. See?"

Mother examined the newspaper photograph of the fragile airplane banking to the left, as elegant as a dragonfly.

"This picture's probably a French fake," Mother said. "I'll believe in airplanes when I see them with my own eyes."

Moe folded the newspaper and sighed. Why was it so difficult to convince some people of things they couldn't see?

To avoid ridicule, Moe kept her dream of flying

a secret from all the world. That was, until she got to know Otto Price.

Otto, who was the same age as Moe, had attended classes with Moe at Mukwanago Elementary since he was five years old. He always sat by himself in a corner in the back of the crowded classroom, where he drew or daydreamed and somehow managed to avoid the attention of overwhelmed Miss Hardwick, whose shrill voice smelled of sour onion. So seldom did Otto speak or answer questions, the other students called him dim-witted. Moe considered him painfully shy, nothing more.

It wasn't until one October afternoon in 1908 that Moe accidentally discovered Otto's hidden talent. At recess she happened to glance at what he was drawing in his sketchbook as he crouched beneath a tree in the schoolyard. Airplanes. Big airplanes, small airplanes. Airplanes banking in hard right turns. Airplanes landing and airplanes pulling straight up into the sky. At that precise moment she realized that she and Otto were both transfixed by the same crazy, outlandish dream that nobody in Luck, Wisconsin, considered the least bit possible.

They became inseparable.

Fall passed. Christmas arrived. Moe's elder sister, Flora, squealed with delight when she opened her gift, a fancy autograph album. Moe didn't find her Christmas present quite so thrilling—a pair of soft kid gloves. What she really wanted was a year's subscription to *Tip Top Weekly,* a magazine that printed thrilling airplane stories. She acted pleased with the ladylike gloves, although deep down she intended to use them only to keep her hands warm when she went out to feed Old Snap, her family's dear, ancient horse.

"Maybe for my twelfth birthday I'll get something really special," Moe confided to Old Snap as she dumped fresh oats into his trough. "Maybe a set of stereoscopic views of the Wright brothers flying. You know the kind I mean. You put them in the viewer and hold it up to the light so that you can see the pictures. They look as real as anything."

Old Snap snorted and chomped mouthfuls of his breakfast. He was interested in oats, not airplanes.

When Moe's birthday arrived, she was again disappointed. This time her gift was an ebony comb and hairbrush set. "To keep your hair neat and tidy," Mother said. Moe thanked her, all the time wondering how far the comb and hairbrush might fly if she threw them out the window.

Mercifully, spring returned, and school ended. Summer seemed to stretch into forever like one long, languorous promise. With Mother away at the Women's Christian Temperance Convention in Milwaukee and Father busily tinkering with the Model T, Moe decided that this particular afternoon in mid-June was the perfect time for Otto to help her get to work on a spectacular plan to celebrate the one-year anniversary of Art Taylor's triumph.

Everything would have worked out just fine if it had not been for fourteen-year-old Flora, who was left in charge while Mother was away. Flora ushered Moe into the parlor, a room ordinarily off limits to the four McDonohugh girls. Flora royally seated herself on the best overstuffed chair beside the round table filled with shadow boxes and glass domes of arranged dried flowers, seeds, and shells. She motioned to Moe to sit on the little needlework stool.

Moe refused. She shifted from one foot to the other, certain that at any moment she would accidentally shatter Mother's porcelain shepherdess statue or knock over the china cuspidor that had been handpainted with posies.

Flora cleared her throat. "I wish you wouldn't associate with that Otto boy."

"His name's Otto Price, not Otto boy, and he happens to be my best friend."

"He's a daredevil," Flora said. She crossed her ankles as if to admire her polished high-button boots. "He has strange habits. Cavorting around town on that bicycle he made. Collecting bats and snakes and other vicious animals. I even hear he keeps a hawk. Is that wise?"

Moe clenched her fist. She wanted to punch her sister, but what would Father say if she gave Flora a black eye?

Flora folded her arms and pursed her thin lips. Her dark hair and pale, critical expression reminded Moe of Mother.

"Just look at yourself, Madeline Genevieve McDonohugh," Flora said, using the full, proper name Moe despised. "Your hair is uncombed. Your dress is stained and wrinkled. And where are your shoes? This is what happens when you spend too much time in that old shed with that odd boy."

"It's not a shed. It's a laboratory and observatory. All scientists need their own space to work. And Otto isn't odd. He's brilliant. He needs me to help him with something important."

Flora's eyes narrowed. "What?"

"It's a surprise." To avoid her sister's glare, Moe stared at the lace curtains billowing in the window. Only two weeks until the Fourth of July. She drummed her fingers against the ornamented head of the gleaming sewing machine Mother had ordered from Sears, Roebuck for nineteen dollars and fifty-five cents.

"And another thing. Your fingernails are unspeakable. Whatever happened to those nice gloves Mother bought for you?" Flora droned. "As for your complexion, if you don't start wearing a hat when you go out in the sun, you know what will happen to your skin. . . ."

With her toe, Moe nudged the sewing machine's wrought-iron pedal. She liked the pleasant squeaking noise the pedal made when the dressmaker came in the spring to sew all their clothes.

"Are you listening to me?" Flora demanded.

"Of course," Moe said. She studied the decorative leaves and flowers that surrounded the word "Minnesota" painted in gold on the sewing machine. Mother was very proud of the mirrorlike finish on the sewing machine's golden oak cabinet. Slyly, Moe slid open the cabinet's top drawer, which contained a pincushion stuffed with dried rose petals. The smell reminded her of Grandmother's fragrant attic full of drying herbs. She slipped out a paper packet that said "Reliable Sewing Machine needles in Assorted Sizes, American No. 7, Philadelphia, PA."

"... And as for the way in which you keep your stockings—"

"Say, Flora," Moe interrupted, "can I borrow these?"

"Do you see what I mean about manners? How will you survive in polite society? You must say, '*May* I borrow—' "

"I'm in a hurry. Otto's waiting."

"You're being very mysterious." Flora stood up and plucked the packet of needles from Moe's hand before Moe could stop her. Flora waved the packet in the air. "Why are you suddenly so interested in sewing? I didn't even know you could thread a needle."

Moe ignored her older sister's smirk. "I need the needles for the sewing machine Otto borrowed from a neighbor. We're punching holes across the middle of the tickets we're making. When the audience comes, we'll tear the tickets in half and let people keep the part that says 'Admit One.' These tickets are going to look really authentic."

"Why do you need such authentic tickets?"

"For our Medicine Show."

Flora groaned. "Last time you nearly started yourself on fire."

"We're not performing a fire-eating act. We're just going to do some comedy routines and some

11

animal exhibits and sell the Elixir of Youth. Otto's made up gallons of colored sugar water. Father gave us a whole box of old, empty bottles from the store, and they're much more interesting than the Wizard Oil bottles they sell when the real Medicine Show comes to town on the train."

"Why can't you make the tickets here? Why must you take the sewing machine needles across town?"

Moe crept close to her sister. "Because," she said in a low voice, "I have some other secret sewing to finish. Something I'm making with some very nice sateen. I'm sure Mother would approve. Sewing is very ladylike." She grabbed the packet and raced to the door. "Thanks again, Flora. Good-bye."

"Make sure you bring every needle back in perfect condition!" Flora called angrily. "Do you hear me?"

Moe tucked the packet into her pocket. She leapt down the front steps two at a time and grabbed a burlap sack hidden under a yew bush in the front yard. She swung the sack over her shoulder and raced toward Main Street, delighted at last to have made her escape.

Chapter 2

Moe envied Otto's freedom. Nobody ever told him to comb his hair or wear a hat or keep track of his gloves. He was lucky. He didn't have an older sister, and he didn't have a mother.

Whenever the subject of Mrs. Price's whereabouts came up at Mother's Sunshine Bible Club, Moe noticed that the ladies clucked and spoke in hushed tones. When Moe asked why, Mother replied, "That's not something I care to discuss." Mrs. Price was not only mysterious, she was famous. A woman with a reputation.

Mr. Price never mentioned his wife. He was so busy running the only furniture and undertaking business in town that he had little time to pay much attention to Otto, the younger of his two sons.

13

Otto's idea of a perfect dinner was to sit under a tree and eat an entire can of tomatoes with a spoon. He wore the same clothing for a week and slept outdoors in a hammock, and nobody hollered. Best of all, Otto was allowed to do whatever he wanted with the tar-papered shed and ramshackle barn in the weedy patch of land behind his father's undertaking business. Otto used the buildings to house a growing menagerie of injured animals that he patiently coaxed back to health. These included an abandoned goat named Melville, assorted stray cats, bats, a snapping turtle, several snakes, a squirrel who answered to the name Dickens, and a fierce red-tailed hawk called Grace. Otto's veterinary skills came in handy on more than one occasion when Old Snap caught a bad cold and had to be cured with a special mustard plaster.

"Otto!" Moe shouted as she staggered breathlessly up to the shed. No one answered. She banged on the laboratory door. Grace flapped in her cage. "I've got the sewing machine needles to make the tickets. Where are you?"

"The roof," Otto said. "Climb up."

Moe tied the bottom of her skirt around her waist so that she could shimmy up the bent apple tree that kept the shed from falling over. The two sides

14

of the roof rose steeply and met at a flattened bowed ridge nearly four feet wide—the perfect spot to observe the hay field and the sky beyond. Under the fierce sun, the sagging tar-paper roof smelled hot and sticky.

Moe sat down beside Otto. He gazed at the sky through his collapsible spyglass. He was short for twelve but wiry and tough. His black hair stood out bristly all over his head. His fingernails were rimmed with sludge, and he so seldom wore shoes that his feet had become as tough as the skin of the elephant Moe had seen at the circus that came through Elkhorn last spring.

"I thought," Moe said, "you were going to make some more Elixir of Youth for the Medicine Show while I was gone."

"Hen hawks rise faster than buzzards, and their motions are steadier."

Moe sighed. "Don't lean so close to the edge. You'll fall."

"And hen hawks don't seem to use much effort to keep their balance. See?" Otto pointed to a spot in the blue sky beyond a flock of clouds and handed Moe the spyglass.

She leaned her skinny elbows on her knees, looked through the spyglass with one eye, and struggled to focus. "Can't spot any hawks," she said. "Did I ever tell you my dream?"

"Look at that!" Otto jumped to his feet and shielded his eyes with his hands. "Just as I thought. The motion of the wings fore and aft is very small."

Moe frowned.

"But when you're standing directly below the hawk, it doesn't seem to draw on one wing more than the other. Now, why is that?"

"How should I know? Really, Otto, don't you want to hear my dream? It was about flying."

Otto sat down. At last she had his complete attention.

"I was walking home from school. Running, actually," she said, and licked her lips with enthusiasm. "I had this hat. It was magic. People followed me. They didn't believe what I could do. I held the hat with both hands, and I waved it up and down in the air. The motion lifted me straight up. I was soaring."

Otto blinked hard. "How did you steer?" he demanded. She could tell that he wasn't making fun of her.

"I think I leaned to the right or the left. Everybody cheered. You should have seen their shocked faces. They didn't believe I could fly."

"How did you land?"

"I can't remember. I woke up too soon."

Otto studied the sky again.

"The dream's a sign," Moe insisted. "We have to finish the airplane so I can be the first girl aeronaut to soar over Luck, Wisconsin, on the Fourth of July. I love that word—*aeronaut*. It sounds so fascinating. Otto, aren't you happy? Now that we have sewing machine needles, we can get the sewing machine running. We can punch holes in the Medicine Show tickets, and we can sew sateen to cover the airplane wings."

"You forgot something important. We don't have any sateen." Otto took a dog-eared notepad from his back pocket. He kept the notepad to list the different species of birds he spotted and other important information. "We've got ninety-seven cents saved so far. We need at least sixteen dollars for two bolts of sateen for the wing fabric and another five dollars for wood for the glider body. And that doesn't include money we'll need for the engine."

"If my plan works, we'll have plenty of money," Moe said. "Wilbur Wright's first flight in public only lasted two minutes. We'll be able to beat that record with your design, don't you think?"

Otto's ears turned bright red, and he looked very pleased.

She gestured grandly to the imaginary crowd cheering them from the ground below. "And when we succeed, think of the publicity! Newspapers from around the country will come to Luck, and they'll interview us. You and me, the youngest fliers in history. Maybe we'll go to Washington, D.C., and shake hands with President William Howard Taft. You could have a real nice conversation."

"What about the twenty-one dollars?"

"We'll make loads of money tomorrow at the Medicine Show. We're going to have real punched tickets. I've put posters up all over town. Everyone's coming except for Grandma Zolnay, who's out of town visiting friends. I'm sure we'll have a huge audience." Moe stood up and brushed off the back of her skirt. "I want to show you something else that's going to make us rich in no time." Expertly, she climbed down the tree. She picked up the sack she'd brought from home and signaled Otto to follow her inside the laboratory.

"Hello, Grace," Moe murmured to the hawk, whose cage took up most of the shed. The fierce-eyed bird stretched her good wing and flapped it so hard, the cage shook.

In the middle of the room was a table covered with pieces of wood from Otto's latest glider model.

Tacked to the wall were countless drawings of airplanes and newspaper clippings about Wilbur and Orville Wright. Wooden crates served as shelves for Otto's fossil and feather collections, Indian clubs, battered books on bird identification, and assorted animal skulls.

"Where's your great discovery?" Otto said as he ducked inside the doorway.

"Here." Dramatically, Moe plunged her hand inside the sack and pulled out something square and black. She hoped she looked as cunning and triumphant as the pilot Frank Merriwell on the cover of the latest issue of *Tip Top Weekly*.

" 'Autographs of Flora McDonohugh,' " Otto read aloud from the cover of the fancy leatherbound book decorated with gold swirls. "You stole your sister's autograph album. How are her classmates' signatures and messages from the last day of school going to make us money?"

Moe smiled. She flipped past the page that said:

When the name that I write here is dim on the page,
And the leaves of your album are yellow with age;
Still think of me kindly, and do not forget
That, wherever I am, I remember you yet.
—Mabel Norquist

Another was penned with:

When on this page you chance to look
Just think of me and close the book.
                    —Your Friend, Agnes

Moe pointed to the two pages at the end, which had been glued together. Written in Flora's best handwriting was the word "Private."

Otto examined the glued pages with a magnifying glass. Then he sniffed them carefully. "A simple paste mixture of flour and water," he said. "Obviously, Flora doesn't want anybody to read what someone wrote here. I don't see the connection with a get-rich-quick scheme."

"Quiet! Someone might be listening," Moe whispered. She took down from a shelf the dusty box containing Otto's "Number Seven Chemistry Set for Edification of Young Scientists." "You are going to invent a special formula to unstick autograph album pages so expertly that no one will ever know that they've been unglued," Moe explained. "Think of the possibilities! Brothers and sisters everywhere will want your formula, which we'll bottle and sell with an attractive label. How does 'Otto's Wonder Unglue' sound? Fifty cents a bottle is a real bargain, don't you think? And we can sell it at the Medicine Show."

"How would you like it if someone took your private messages, unglued the pages, read them, and threatened to tell the whole world?"

Moe scowled. "I'd still like to find out what Flora's page says."

Otto opened his pocketknife, picked up a small piece of wood from the table where he'd been working on the airplane model, and began whittling. His head was bent so low, Moe could not see his face. But she could tell he was flustered. The tips of his ears were red again.

"If you aren't going to help me," she said in a hurt voice, "I'll just invent the Unglue myself." She lifted the lid of the chemistry set, which was filled with little bottles of colored powder and vials of foul-smelling liquid.

"Better be careful," he warned. "You can create a terrible explosion if you don't know what you're doing."

She mixed a pinch of bright green paste with some slimy yellow liquid in a tiny glass beaker. "I *know* what I'm doing," she lied. Ordinarily, a nice, loud explosion would suit Otto just fine. What was wrong with him? She added some black powder.

Nothing happened.

"Any luck?" Otto asked.

Moe shook her head. But she wasn't going to give up. Not now. She tipped the turtle's drinking bowl into her cupped hand and sprinkled droplets on the mixture. It began to sizzle.

"Something's happening!" she said excitedly. Using a stick, she spread a small amount of the mixture on the edges of the page. The black paper turned white, then began to curl. "It's working!" she shouted.

Slowly the pages came unstuck. It was a miracle, really. Moe never expected such good luck on her first try. She waited. Then, gingerly, she lifted the edge of the page and read aloud:

When other lips and other hearts,
their tales of love shall tell . . .
then remember me.
                    —Love always, Ben Price

Moe's jaw dropped.

"I can't believe it," Otto said. His face looked pale even under a layer of grime. "Maybe it's a forgery."

"Does this look like your brother's handwriting?"

Otto nodded.

"Disgusting! How could Ben write something like this to *my* nasty sister?"

"Maybe he just lost his senses on the last day of school. A seizure or something."

"Ben always seemed perfectly normal to me," Moe said sadly. Last year in the dead of night, Ben and his friends took hateful Mr. Simpson's rubber-tired buggy apart, hauled it piece by piece to the top of the water tower, reassembled it, and balanced it atop the fish weather vane. Another time they captured Skunk McPherson, painted him blue, and shoved him into the back of a hearse awaiting a dead body outside the Methodist Church. These deeds were normal. They required nerve and imagination. But writing a poem about lips and hearts in Flora's album? *That* was sick.

"What are we going to do?" Moe pressed the pages back together. "They won't stick. And I'm afraid I won't be able to get rid of that white burned mark along the edge. It looks sort of suspicious, doesn't it?"

"You should have thought of that before you smeared chemicals on the page," Otto said. "I've got some wood glue that might work. But we can't do much about the damage. Maybe you should tell Flora the truth."

Moe frowned. If she told Flora exactly what she'd done, her older sister would surely kill her. "I'll hide the album somewhere," Moe said finally. Wasn't Flora's wrath worse than eternal damnation for lying? "Maybe she'll think she lost it."

"What if some of the boys from the pool hall find the album and read it? Ben will be the laughing-stock of the whole town. He can't tolerate people making fun of him."

Moe stared at Otto in disbelief. Anybody who wrote lovesick poems about hearts and lips deserved to be made fun of.

"Promise me you'll hide the album someplace no-body will ever find it," Otto begged.

"Well, if you're that worried, I'll—"

Suddenly the laboratory door shook with loud, persistent knocking. "Let us in!" someone shouted.

Chapter 3

"My sisters!" Moe hissed.

Otto grabbed the album and slid it beneath a pile of newspapers. He bit his lip, and his eyes bugged out. "What if they find it?"

"They won't," Moe said in a low voice. "Winnie? Pearl?" she called through the closed door. "Is that you?"

The door opened. "We've been looking all over for you, Moe," eight-year-old Winnie said. Winnie and her shadow, seven-year-old Pearl, slipped inside before Moe could stop them. Suddenly the laboratory seemed very crowded.

"Hello, Otto," Winnie said in a shy voice. She looked longingly at the bird in the cage. "How is Grace? Can I feed her?"

"Hello, yourself," Otto grumbled. "I doubt you came all this way to take care of Grace. What do you want?"

"We're here to help," Pearl announced. "Flora told us you're working on the Medicine Show and you need us."

"She did, did she?" Moe replied. Good old Flora.

"Can I be in an act?" Pearl clutched her hand in a fist and thrust it against her forehead. "Oh, wretched state!" she cried. "Oh, bosom black as death!"

"*That* old speech!" Winnie said. "Do you want everyone to cry? I think something funny would be much better. Like this:

"There was an old man of Tarrentum, who sat on his false teeth and bent 'em; when asked what he'd lost, and what they had cost, he replied, 'I don't know, I just rent 'em.' " Winnie howled with laughter. She obviously thought her limerick quite clever.

The Medicine Show, which came every June, was a favorite of Otto, Moe, and her sisters. One of the train cars on the Milwaukee line would pull off the main track onto a separate track. The car housed the Medicine Show performers, who set up a giant tent outside town. For one week there were vaudeville acts and singing and speeches. Hawkers roamed the aisles with bottles of Hamlin's Wizard Oil and Dr. Rose's Dyspepsia Powders.

Each year everyone in town waited for the event. Moe never missed an act, and neither did her sisters. On some days, if Mother and Father let them, Moe, Winnie, and Pearl watched the Medicine Show three times in a row. Naturally, Moe had every line memorized by the time the show left town.

"I don't think we can really use your help," Otto said to the younger girls. He gave Moe a look that meant, *Make them go away.*

Moe shrugged. Otto did not understand the constant, pesky demands of little sisters. He had no idea how much tact and imagination it took to deal with Winnie and Pearl—not unlike handling two lit firecrackers at the same time.

"I have an idea," Moe said brightly. "Why don't you go home and play paper dolls?"

"Paper dolls?" Winnie's bottom lip trembled, as if she were about to burst into tears.

"Paper dolls are dumb," Pearl said. "We want to be in the show. Flora said we could."

Moe scowled. "She never asked me."

"We're not lying," Pearl insisted. "She said, 'Tell Moe to let you help, or she has to give back the sewing machine needles.' That's exactly what she said, isn't it, Winnie?"

Winnie nodded vigorously. "She said if we came back home and bothered her one more time, she'd march right out here and make you put us in the show."

Moe groaned. Suddenly she didn't feel so terrible about ruining her bossy sister's album. Flora deserved worse. If she showed up, she'd ruin everything. So far she'd never once ventured inside Otto's laboratory. Neither had Father. Winnie and Pearl, young and stupid, with faces pink as babies' knees, were the only ones who had ever been allowed inside, because Moe figured they didn't know enough to criticize or ridicule. Not yet, anyway.

"All right," Moe said, nudging Otto with her elbow. Desperate cooperation was better than complete defeat. "You two can help us."

Otto glanced at the pile of newspapers that hid the album. "As long as you never bring Flora here and you never tell anyone about what you see here," he grumbled. "This place is very secret."

"Oh!" Pearl gushed. "I'm good at secrets. Isn't that so, Moe? I never told anyone about your valentine from Martin Heeley or—"

Moe clamped her hand over her sister's mouth.

"You can count on me. I'm eight and three-quarters, and I know how to keep secrets," Winnie said in a superior voice.

Moe lifted her hand away from Pearl's mouth. "I'll keep quiet!" Pearl sputtered, red-faced.

"If you tell anyone anything, you can never come here again as long as you live," Moe said.

"Don't send me back to Flora!" Pearl pleaded. "I won't tell anyone. You're my favorite sister, Moe."

Moe rolled her eyes.

"What are we going to do first?" Winnie asked.

"First thing we're going to do is set up the stage in the barn," Moe announced. "Isn't that right, Otto?"

Otto nodded reluctantly.

"We've already moved out the old buggy and wheels and barrels," Moe said. "You know how to sweep?"

Winnie and Pearl nodded with great enthusiasm. "Of course!"

"Then you take these brooms," Moe said, "and get to work sweeping the area in front of the open barn door. That's where we're going to set up benches for the audience."

The rest of the afternoon Otto, Moe, and her sisters worked to get the theater ready. The ramshackle barn leaned dangerously to one side ever since the last big windstorm, but Moe wasn't afraid to go inside. She held a broom up by its handle and cleared away cobwebs. Of course, she knew the spiders were probably still hiding somewhere else in the barn. But somehow the broom waving gave Otto, who loathed spiders, enough courage to go inside to string the shabby quilt in the doorway as a stage curtain.

Moe helped her sisters lift long, rough boards atop barrels and boxes to make benches. She carefully poked each ticket that said "Admit One" with the sewing machine to make the lovely holes like tickets at the real Medicine Show. Otto arranged the cages and crates on the shady side of the barn for the animal display. The last animal he moved was Grace. Carefully he dragged her cage outside through the laboratory door.

"Can I feed Grace?" Winnie asked.

"No," Otto replied. "She only eats from my hand."

"What do you feed her?"

"Fresh dead mice."

Winnie made a squeamish face.

Otto pulled on a pair of thick leather gloves that were far too big for him. He ducked and crawled inside Grace's cage, which had been made from screen doors and sections of old wire fence. He moved slowly and whistled softly. "Hello, Grace," he said quietly. The huge hawk stared at him with her golden-orb eyes. She seemed to be able to look right through him. Her chest was white, speckled with brown feathers. And her wings were a warm brownish red. She preened her feathers with her sharp beak and lifted one foot, displaying her razor-sharp talons. Then she curled her long toes and tucked one leg under herself.

"Wake up now, Grace," Otto said in a low voice. "I've got something special for you." He stretched out his gloved hand and used the other to pull a dead mouse from his pocket. He draped the mouse over his gloved hand. "It's tasty. Come see."

Grace's golden eyes seemed to swallow up Otto the same way somebody might gulp a tall glass of cold water on a hot day. She spread her massive wings and flapped twice. In a rush of brown and white, she swooped and landed on Otto's gloved wrist. She gripped the limp mouse in one claw and, with her beak, tore off its head.

Winnie clamped her hands over her eyes. "I can't watch."

"How did you expect her to eat—with a knife

and fork?" Otto asked. Quickly, Grace swallowed another piece of mouse. Then she flew back to her perch. Gripping a piece of mouse in her talons, she turned and hid her meal beneath her outstretched wings.

"Why is she hiding her food from us like that?" Winnie demanded.

"It's called mantling. Maybe she does it because she thinks you might steal her food."

"But I don't want her dead mouse," Winnie said. "How did you teach her to come to your hand like that?"

Otto shrugged. "Practice, I guess. It took months for her to learn. But don't you ever try it. Without the heavy glove, her claws would go right through your skin."

Winnie nodded grimly, as if she had no intention of trying to feed Grace.

"What should we say on our sign?" Moe asked. "How about 'Flesh-eating Hawk'? That sounds catchy."

"All hawks are flesh-eating," Otto replied.

Moe sighed. "Otto, we're just trying to come up with a name that will be sure to attract a crowd." She scribbled the words on a piece of board, which she leaned against Grace's cage. "The unicorn's ready. Take a look. It's really spectacular."

Otto gasped when he saw the rolled paper cone attached to the middle of the goat's forehead with a piece of elastic. Melville didn't seem to enjoy his starring role as unicorn. He stuck out his enormous tongue and tried to eat the new horn. When that didn't work, he shook his head in a dismal, hopeless fashion. "Remove that thing right this minute," Otto demanded.

"Why?"

"It's humiliating."

"All right," Moe said impatiently. "Here's the snapping turtle. It's pretty boring unless somebody sticks a finger in its crate."

"Then what happens?" Pearl asked.

"The turtle bites it off," Moe said.

"Oh," Pearl replied in a little voice.

"The bats won't do much this time of day except sleep," Moe complained. "I wish you'd let me call the snakes pythons or king cobras. Poisonous snakes are much more interesting."

"Garter snakes are not venomous," Otto said.

Moe sighed. Sometimes Otto's constant effort to be truthful could be very tiresome.

"Aren't we going to work on our acts?" Winnie asked.

"We know them by heart," Moe said. "But we do need to work on costumes. That's going to be your big job, Winnie and Pearl."

Winnie's face brightened. "I'm very good at finding things. What do you need?"

"A couple fancy hats," Moe said. "A pair of bright trousers with suspenders. A lady's scarf. Some beads. You know, the usual. We're doing the German Act. We also need a pie pan and some flour."

"That shouldn't be hard. Ella has the day off. It'll be easy to sneak into the kitchen," Winnie said happily. "I have to get my costume ready, too. I have my act all planned."

"Me, too," Pearl said.

"All right. Hurry along. Just don't let Flora catch you," Moe said. "Remember, the performance is tomorrow. We don't have much time." She motioned for her sisters to be on their way. They scurried out of sight.

"Do your sisters always talk so much?" Otto asked in a weary voice.

"Sometimes," Moe admitted, "they talk more."

Chapter 4

Children from town gathered in Otto's yard at two o'clock the next day. A few tired, wailing toddlers were led by the hand by older, frowning sisters. Winnie collected pennies and tore tickets. Moe peeked around the stage curtain so that she could watch the audience's faces as they filed onto the benches. To her disappointment, no one seemed the least bit impressed by the authentic-looking tickets she had worked so hard to make.

"Here's the last of the Elixir of Youth," Otto said. He poured the remaining colored sugar water into a bottle. "I thought I poured a dozen yesterday. Now they're empty. Strange." Otto scratched his chin. He was wearing a large beard cut from the pieces of an old Santa wig.

Pearl burped and then spun on her toes. "How do I look?" She had tied one of Mother's old scarves about her waist and wore glass beads around her neck and an ostrich plume behind her ear. In one hand she carried a fancy lace fan taken from Mother's bureau drawer.

"I'm not sure Mother would be happy to see so many of her things onstage," Moe said.

"I'll take good care of these scarves," Pearl promised. She daubed her face with flour to give it a pale color.

"Do you know anything about missing Elixir of Youth?" Moe asked suspiciously.

Pearl shook her head. "No. Why are you looking at me so mean? I didn't do nothing."

"Just make sure of that," Moe said. She peered out from behind the curtain again and began counting. ". . . Twenty, twenty-one, twenty-two—plus the Cranes' dog, Mercy. We're going to be rich!"

Nervously Otto fumbled with the caps on the last bottles of Elixir. "These fancy pants your sister found are too tight. I can hardly move," he complained. The bright green trousers he wore had been sewn two years ago by Mother as part of Moe's elf costume for a school pageant. "Maybe I should just wear my own trousers."

"They look very bright and theatrical," Moe insisted. "You're supposed to be a foreigner in the act. I think they're wonderful. Besides, there isn't time to change. You've got to get out there and sell some Elixir." Moe pushed Otto out from behind the curtain with a box of bottles.

"Elixir of Youth! Five cents!" he shouted.

"Ten cents!" Moe whispered from behind the curtain.

"Elixir of Youth! Ten cents!" Otto called.

"That's too much for some dumb bottle!" someone in the audience called out.

"What's in that stuff anyhow?"

"Special ingredients. Try it, and you'll stay young forever!" Otto promised. "Never have to grow up and burp screaming babies. Never wear a stiff collar to church. Never have to get a job and get married and die!"

Three Feeney brothers hooted their approval. "I'll buy a bottle!" one shouted. He unscrewed the top and took a sip. "Tastes good. It's sweet as anything."

From backstage came the sound of sobbing. "Now what's wrong with you?" Moe asked Pearl. The little girl crouched on the floor, held her stomach, and rocked back and forth.

"I don't want to be seven years old forever!" she wailed.

"How many bottles did you drink?" Moe demanded.

Pearl sniffed. "Six."

"Six!" Moe exclaimed.

"Does that mean I'll never grow up and get to wear a long taffeta dress?"

Moe groaned. Sometimes she couldn't believe how perfectly stupid her sisters could be.

"We want the show! We want the show!" the audience called, stomping on the ground.

Moe signaled to Otto and her sisters for the show to begin. "The first act," she whispered, "is the German routine."

"No!" Winnie insisted. "The burning deck's first. You said I could go first. I'm ready." Winnie pouted. She had arranged her sailor costume and had even decorated her face with smudges of charcoal from the cinder bin behind the house. "I even have some special surprises for the piece."

"What surprises?" Moe asked.

"You'll see," Winnie said eagerly. "Just let me go on before I get scared and forget all the words."

Moe clucked her tongue. Liar! Winnie had never

had stage fright in her life. "Get out there before everybody goes home."

By taking very small steps, Otto managed to push open the curtain. Winnie marched onstage in an enormous coat that had once belonged to Grandfather when he was in the Navy. The audience clapped and whistled.

Winnie struck a tragic pose. Her chin jutted out, and she held her hands clasped together in front of 'her chest. " 'Casabianca,' by Felicia Dorothea Hemans," she said in a loud voice.

"Who's she?" someone called.

"Never heard of her!" someone else hooted.

Winnie gave the audience an intense glare. She cleared her throat and said in a commanding voice: "The boy stood on the burning deck, whence all but he had fled . . ." She swayed back and forth. As she did so, she slipped one hand inside her pocket and pulled out a deck of cards.

"Where did she get those?" Otto asked, peeking from backstage.

Moe shrugged. Mother did not allow card playing.

Determinedly Winnie continued: "The flames rolled on; he would not go without his father's word." She put her hand inside her other pocket and produced a box of matches. Moe held her

breath as her sister lit the deck of cards with the match and threw them onto the barn floor.

"There came a burst of thunder sound; the boy—oh! Where was he?"

The crowd cheered. Cards smoldered at Winnie's feet. She lifted her long trouser legs and was about to step directly into the flames when Moe rushed out from backstage. She shoved her sister out of the way, stomped on the cards, and put them out with help from Otto, who poured the remaining Elixir on the fire. The crowd booed, clearly upset at being deprived of the right to see Winnie burst into flames.

"What do you think you're doing?" Otto demanded angrily.

"Standing on a burning deck," Winnie replied.

"Don't you know anything?" Moe asked, furious that her sister could be so ignorant. "The poem's about a *ship's* deck, not a deck of *cards!*"

"Oh," Winnie said in a small voice.

"We want the show! We want the show!" The audience bellowed and stomped their feet.

"Shut the curtain," Moe hissed to Otto.

He painfully made his way across the stage again, pulling the curtain behind him. "Act Two," he announced.

Moe kicked the last piece of charred card out of the way. She pulled to the middle of the stage a table with a pan filled with flour. "Ready?" she said, tying a kerchief around her head. "Curtain!"

Otto opened the curtain. "The German Act."

The crowd cheered. Everyone knew the German Act. Moe played the wife. Otto took the part of the husband. She shook her fist at him. He shook his fist at her. Since neither knew German, they shouted at each other using the only phrase they had ever heard:

"Ach du Lieber Augustine?"

"Ach du Lieber Augustine!"

Moe pounded Otto on the back. Just like the real Medicine Show act, she tried to push his bearded face into the pan of flour. But his pants were so tight he could not bend.

"What'll we do?" Moe whispered frantically.

"Lift the pan," Otto hissed.

Moe lifted the pan and hit Otto on the head. The flour went everywhere—his hair, his beard, his eyebrows. He blinked in a cloud of white. The crowd cheered. Otto sputtered. Before he and Moe could take a bow, a horrible shriek filled the air.

"War! War!" Rotten crab apples shot against the

curtain and bounced off the barn door. *Ping! Ping! Ping!*

"It's the Highview gang!" Otto shouted. Moe ducked behind the table. The audience scattered, screaming.

The filthy Highview invaders swarmed the theater and knocked over benches. The vicious dozen, who came to school shoeless except during the coldest weeks of the year, lived in shanties east of the railroad tracks. They were tough outcasts, prone to head lice. Nobody spoke to them. Nobody sat near them. Their attacks were always unpredictable and fueled by powerful, defiant rage.

"Go away!" Winnie cried. "You're ruining everything."

A big Highview boy, who had decorated his face with streaks of red paint, jumped and tore down the curtain. Another gleefully smashed the bottles of Elixir of Youth. A few others toppled the table with the punched tickets and trampled the costumes. They scrambled around the barn, pelting the remaining members of the audience with crab apples.

Bellowing a victory whoop, the attackers knocked sticks against the frantic animals' cages. And then, in the midst of the screams and pelting crab apples, one of the Highview boys made a big mistake.

He unlocked Grace's door.

The furious bird exploded from the cage. She spread her wings, powerful talons gleaming. For several moments the Highview boys did not know what to do. They stood trembling.

"KEEEE-aahr-rrrr!" Grace shrieked.

"Watch out!" the boys screamed.

The hawk flapped. She circled once, twice over their heads. The Highview boys raised their arms over their faces to protect themselves. They raced away in terror, screaming as loudly as if the hawk had actually sunk her sharp beak into their spines.

Grace circled a third time and made a clumsy landing on the roof of her cage. She was breathing hard, her chest expanding with each breath. She extended her wings and gave a contented flap.

"Good girl," Otto murmured. "It's all right. They're gone now. Go back inside your house."

The bird awkwardly walked across the top of the cage and managed to lower herself into the open doorway. She bobbed and made a big jump, landing on her perch.

"Did you see that?" Winnie said quietly.

"She saved us," Pearl said.

Miserably, Moe surveyed the toppled benches,

spilled flour, and broken bottles. "Did they get the money?"

Winnie patted her pocket and grinned. "Don't worry. I hid it. We still have lots and lots."

"Good for you!" Moe said. Maybe her sister was good for something after all.

Winnie emptied her pocket on the ground. When Moe counted the pennies, she discovered that the Medicine Show profits were exactly thirty-six cents.

"We're rich!" Pearl crooned.

Otto moaned. "Not quite."

"We can't give up," Moe said as cheerfully as she could. "We'll think of another way to come up with more money."

"I've got lots of ideas," Pearl announced. "What about fishing for lost change between boardwalk cracks? All we need is a piece of chewing gum on the end of a long stick and—"

"Stop!" Otto bellowed. "I can't stand it! Don't say another word." He stomped inside the laboratory and slammed the door.

"What's the matter with him?" Winnie asked, surprised.

"Too much talking," Moe said, and sighed.

Chapter 5

The afternoon after the disastrous Medicine Show, Moe knew she had to keep moving or bust.

"Let's go somewhere. Anywhere," she announced to her two sisters, who had forgotten all about the tragedy and were busy studying a bucket of water outside Otto's lab. "What are you doing?"

"We put a hair from a horse's tail in the water, and we're waiting for it to turn into an eel," Winnie explained in a wise voice.

"Whoever heard of such rubbish? Horse hairs don't turn into eels," Moe said.

"Yes they do," Pearl insisted. "We just got to wait here till it starts swimming around."

"You two are fools," Moe muttered. "I'm going

for a walk into town. You want to come with me or go home?"

"We want to go with you!" Winnie said. "Can Melville come, too? He looks so lonely. Can we take him on a walk?"

"Say yes, Moe!" Pearl exclaimed. "And let him pull his little cart. He loves to pull his little cart."

"I don't care," Moe said, "as long as it's all right with you, Otto."

Otto grunted. For the past half hour he'd been sitting at the table in the laboratory staring at the model of their airplane without saying a word. That was the problem with being brilliant, Moe decided. Sometimes no amount of cheering and cajoling could lift a genius out of a dark mood.

"Otto, you can just stay here with the horse hair floating in the bucket," Moe said in exasperation. She pulled from behind the shed the little rubber-wheeled cart that Otto had made with old bicycle tires. Then she harnessed the goat to the cart. "All right. Let's go."

Winnie and Pearl still weren't ready to leave. They'd decided that Melville needed to wear the sailor hat that Winnie had worn in the Medicine Show. Pearl tied the hat around his head and held it in place with a long scarf to keep the sun out of the goat's eyes.

Moe started walking. She shoved her hands into the pockets of her long skirt and kept her eyes on her feet. Next came her sisters, prancing in front of Melville for encouragement. Nimbly the goat trotted along, unashamed of his ridiculous headgear.

The sun shone. The sky between the trees was bright blue. But Moe couldn't appreciate the weather. She was lost in thought. How would they ever come up with enough money to build the airplane?

"Who's that?" Winnie called out.

Moe looked up. In Luck, everyone knew everything about everybody. That was just the way it was in a small town where even every dog could be identified by name. The stranger loped past the Buena Vista House and Humphery's Dry Goods and Price Evans Furniture and Undertaking. As he came closer, Moe noticed that his dusty shoes were so worn, shabby yellow socks poked through gaps in the leather.

"Hello," Moe said in a friendly manner. Her sisters held on to Melville's bridle so he wouldn't bolt away or do some other rude thing. The stranger wiped the back of his long sunburned neck with a

49

grimy handkerchief. He was a tall man. The black, bulky object strapped over one shoulder made him lean to one side like a fence post after a blizzard.

"You be citizens of this fine town?" he asked.

Moe nodded, still staring at his socks.

"I don't usually walk everywhere. My buggy's being repaired. Axle broke. You must know lots of folks hereabouts."

Moe nodded.

"Know anybody who needs their photograph taken? Not the Brownie snapshot variety but a real professional photograph." He tucked two bony fingers inside his vest pocket and pulled out a grubby card. "The name's Howard Weeks."

Moe read the card. It said "Photographer. Specializing in Timeless Portraits of Babies, Children, and Other Loved Ones. Reasonable." Moe handed back the card.

"Charming goat and cart you've got there," Mr. Weeks said, looking over Melville, who nibbled the edge of the scarf. "I could sure use something like that for publicity. People are always looking for something unusual in photos these days. It's not enough to roll down a seascape backdrop or set up some fancy wicker chair. Ever consider renting out your goat and cart?"

"Depends," Moe said, wondering what Otto might say. "How much you willing to pay?" She had never considered that anyone would be interested in ill-mannered Melville. While the goat was behaving very nicely at the moment, he had a natural attraction to trouble.

"I'll pay a quarter for every customer who poses in the cart."

"A whole quarter?" Moe said in amazement. They'd be rich in no time! And wouldn't Otto be delighted by the news?

Winnie tugged on the back of Moe's skirt. "What about us? We can knock on doors. Can't we, Pearl?"

"Sure, sure," Moe said, imagining how they'd arrive at the laboratory with their pockets bulging with money. "My name's Madeline Genevieve McDonohugh. But everyone calls me Moe. These are my sisters, Pearl and Winnie."

"Pleased to meet you," Mr. Weeks said, smiling. "I was beginning to be worried about business in your fair city. But now I can see that we're about to embark on a famous partnership. Which house would you say is a worthy place for us to begin?"

Moe looked up and down the block. She pointed to the gray house with the stone foundation and the white picket fence. "Mrs. Eastman has another new baby. Why not try her first?"

Mr. Weeks brushed off his coat and set his camera equipment on the sidewalk. He walked determinedly up the front steps and knocked on the door. Unfortunately Mrs. Eastman did not want her baby's photo taken. Neither did Mrs. Harcourt, Mrs. Crane, or Mrs. Critchfield.

Instead of seeming to be discouraged by so many refusals, Mr. Weeks appeared more enthusiastic than ever.

"I'm sure the next person will say yes," he said energetically.

Moe trudged behind Mr. Weeks. Her sisters dragged exhausted Melville down the street. They had completely lost interest in being photographic assistants. Pearl climbed into the buggy. Winnie complained she was hungry. Moe was hungry, too. She sniffed pot roast and onions coming from Mrs. Dudley's house.

"How about this house?" Mr. Weeks asked.

"That's the Dillards'," Winnie said in a doubtful voice. "They just had twins."

"Why didn't you say so earlier?" Mr. Weeks rubbed his hands together. He straightened his shoulders and marched up the front steps of the peeling green house with the wheelless wagon propped upside down in the yard. The Dillards' mangy, blind dog, Trixie, barked once from beneath the wagon and went back to sleep. Melville paid no attention to the mongrel. He nibbled dandelions along what was left of the Dillards' unpainted fence.

Mr. Weeks knocked loudly. No answer. He knocked again.

"Hello?" Mrs. Dillard said, opening the door a crack. "Who are you?"

"The name's Howard Weeks, Photographer. I've heard that a beautiful set of twins resides here and that you are the lucky mother. I was wondering if you'd like to have the darling children's photograph taken."

"Who told you they was darling?" Mrs. Dillard said. She opened the door wider. Her colorless eyes appeared sunken in her fleshy cheeks. She wiped her hands on her stained apron and slipped one foot out of her backless slipper to rub the back of her leg.

Moe waved. She jabbed her sisters so they waved, too. "Hello, Mrs. Dillard," Moe called. "How are you today?"

"Tolerable, except for the ringworm. What you

doing with that buggy and goat?" she called in her booming voice that could be used at suppertime to summon her five sons from more than three blocks away.

"I'm glad you asked," Mr. Weeks chimed in. "The buggy's the perfect place to set up a unique picture. Imagine how delighted your relatives will be to receive a photograph with your sweet infants sitting in a goat-driven buggy. Charming, don't you think?"

Mrs. Dillard's face collapsed into a skeptical expression. "My babies aren't that good-looking."

Mr. Weeks cocked his head in a friendly manner. "Every baby's beautiful in his own way. I'm sure your twins are priceless. Besides, we can set the camera back a bit for the photo."

"How much you charge?"

"For you, two dollars. That's a good deal. And I'll have photos ready for you in a week's time."

"Two whole dollars? That's a lot for two little babies who weigh hardly more than a sack of flour together."

"I'm certain your sweet children are worth two dollars. You know how fleeting life is. We must treasure every moment of precious childhood."

Moe thought Mr. Weeks might burst into tears at

any moment, he seemed so overwrought with emotion. But Mrs. Dillard didn't appear to be the least impressed. "Sorry, can't really spend two dollars on Davey and Duane. Now if they was girls, maybe I'd reconsider. But all my boys look alike at this age. They take after their father. And I already got one baby picture of the oldest around here somewheres, I think. No need to spend two dollars just to get a goat and buggy in the picture. Good-bye." She started to close the door.

Quickly Mr. Weeks slid his foot in the doorway. "One dollar."

She opened the door and peered out. "Fifty cents."

"Seventy-five. That's my final offer."

"Done," Mrs. Dillard said. "Now I've got to round them up. You just put your camera over yonder. I'll be right back with the boys."

When Mr. Weeks turned, Moe could see the expression of disappointment on his face. His shoulders slumped forward. For the first time, she noticed that his suit was so thin, his bony shoulder blades seemed to be poking through.

"It's a start at least," she said in an encouraging voice. "I'm sure you'll think of something real artistic to do with Davey and Duane. Where should we set up?"

"How about over there?" Mr. Weeks suggested. He pointed to a wild hedge of hollyhocks and day-lilies, the only green patch in the hardscrabble yard.

Winnie and Pearl tugged Melville to the spot. By now the goat had eaten the sailor hat. He stood among broken crates and rusty cans and chewed what stems of grass he could find.

The back door suddenly swung open. Out marched Mrs. Dillard with a red-faced baby under each of her fat arms. The babies squawked so loudly, Moe's ears throbbed.

"They look like the wrong ends of two pigs," Winnie said.

Moe jabbed her hard with her elbow. "Shut up and hold the goat so he doesn't bolt."

While Mrs. Dillard fussed with the babies in the cart, Mr. Weeks positioned his camera so that the bright sunlight was at his back. The twins cried so constantly, Moe wondered how they managed to breathe.

"You think they look better in bonnets?" Mrs. Dillard boomed over the noise. Duane and Davey screamed and squirmed and flopped to one side.

Their pudgy arms flailed in the air like the legs of a well-fed tick flipped on its back.

"Maybe the picture'd look better if you could see their hair," Moe shouted.

Mrs. Dillard removed one of the bonnets. She licked her hand and brushed it against the top of the bald baby's scalp as if to rough up a ridge of hair. The babies hollered louder.

"See what I mean? All my boys is homely this age. It's those ears," she said, and tied the bonnet back on.

Moe had to agree that the ugly babies looked better with bonnets. But she smiled and nodded politely. By this time, Melville was getting agitated from so much crying. He pawed the ground and yanked the harness.

"I think I'll get them into their christening outfits. That'll look better, don't you think?" Mrs. Dillard asked. She tucked the babies under her arms and shuffled into the house.

Mr. Weeks wiped the back of his neck, then shook his head. "That goat looks mighty hot. Why don't you unhook him and walk him around to the front where it's shady before he collapses?"

Moe helped Winnie unharness the goat. Pearl insisted on holding the harness and leading Melville into the front of the house. Mr. Weeks sat under a tree, tipped his hat over his bony face, and soon appeared to be asleep.

Moe scowled. This was not the booming business she had hoped for. It might be hours before they finished taking the picture of the Dillard twins. And all she was going to get out of it was one quarter!

Finally Mrs. Dillard reappeared with the babies. Now they were wearing long gowns blotched yellow in the front. Because the christening outfits were several sizes too small, the babies squirmed and screamed even more. "These outfits have been in my family for years," Mrs. Dillard boasted. "It will just tickle my mother to see them. Now, where's the goat?"

Mr. Weeks leapt to his feet, still groggy from his nap. "Moe? Can you locate the animal?"

Moe hurried to the front of the house. "Winnie! Pearl! Melville!" she called. "Where are you?" She searched the bushes. No sisters. No goat. She found a rope tied to a scrawny tree. The rope appeared to have been nibbled on one end. Had the goat escaped? A gust of wind blew open the torn screen door. Moe rushed up the front steps. "Melville?" she called frantically into the doorway. Mother had always told her not to enter someone's house without asking first. But this was an emergency. "Melville! Come here."

As soon as Moe stepped inside, she wished she hadn't. The overpowering smell of boiled cabbage, soiled diapers, and wet dog made her gag. Carefully she tried to breathe through her mouth as she tiptoed around broken chairs, heaps of clothing, mismatched shoes, a rifle, a box of cartridges, and a rusty saw. "Melville?" she called softly. She pushed open a door. There was Mrs. Dillard's parlor, the only room in the house that didn't seem to be damaged. Standing in the middle of a garish rag rug was Melville, happily munching on a lace doily he had pulled from the arm of the dark purple sofa.

"Stop!" Moe shouted. She pulled the lace doily from the goat's teeth. That's when she noticed that the ferns had been cropped short, the set of lopsided candles had been bitten in half, and stuffing was spilling out of the cushion embroidered with "Mother Dearest."

Melville looked up from the damage without a trace of guilt on his shaggy face. Moe pushed the goat, putting all her weight behind him. Then she pulled the rope and finally managed to drag him out the front door and down the steps—just as she heard a terrible wailing, louder than ten sets of screaming twins.

"What," Mrs. Dillard bellowed, "was that creature doing in my house?"

Chapter 6

The purple-faced babies were so startled by their mother's outburst, they forgot to shriek. Mrs. Dillard thrust the twins into Moe's arms and rushed into the house.

"Oh, no. Oh, no," Mr. Weeks repeated over and over.

Moe couldn't bear to look him straight in the eye. The babies squirmed and twisted like frisky nightcrawlers. So that she didn't drop them on their heads, she placed them carefully on the ground at the bottom of the front steps. Contentedly, the twins ate fistfuls of dirt.

Mrs. Dillard exploded out the front door, her face filled with fury. "My best room! Why'd you let a goat in there? I don't even let my husband in the parlor!"

"No need to be upset, Mrs. Dillard," Mr. Weeks said. "This unfortunate damage will of course be paid for by the owner of the animal." He glared at Moe.

Moe bit her lip and gave Melville's rope a hard tug. "It's not my fault. My sisters were supposed to be watching him, but they left. He got loose and wandered into your house—"

"You'll pay for this," Mrs. Dillard interrupted, "or I'll get the sheriff. You hear?"

"Now, now," Mr. Weeks said nervously. "No need to go to extremes. I'm sure we can solve this problem in an amicable way. How about that photo? And I'm sure Moe will pay to replace your— your—"

"My cushion, my fern, my lace doily," Mrs. Dillard said angrily. "That's at least five dollars' worth of quality merchandise."

Moe frowned. Nothing in Mrs. Dillard's parlor was quality merchandise. And certainly nothing was worth five whole dollars. How was Moe going to come up with that kind of money?

"Now let's get a quick photo," Mr. Weeks said. He plucked the filthy babies up from the dirt and plopped them in the buggy. Quickly he set up his camera. This time Duane and Davey didn't scream.

"Give their faces a wipe," Mr. Weeks said. "That's it. Now smile ... smile ... *smile!* Thank you, Mrs. Dillard. Your picture will be ready next week, and I'm sure Miss Moe will pay you back, or you may speak with her parents. Isn't that right, Moe?"

Moe nodded hopelessly. She watched Mrs. Dillard storm inside her house with the babies and slam the door. "Mr. Weeks, sir," Moe pleaded. "What about my quarter?"

"Considering the damage your goat's caused, I hardly see the point in paying you. However, since I'm an honest man, I'll give you my personal IOU." He took one of his business cards from his pocket and scribbled on the back with a flourish. "You'll get your quarter when Mrs. Dillard pays for her picture." He tipped his hat, lifted his camera to his shoulder, and walked quickly in the direction of the train station.

Moe knew she'd never see the quarter. She knew she'd never see Mr. Weeks again. She folded the card in half and fed it to Melville. Her problem was Mrs. Dillard, the one person she *would* see again, everywhere she went in Luck. Moe picked up the goat's rope and trudged down the street. Now what? Not only had she not made any money, but she owed money she didn't have. What would Otto say when he found out? And what would Mother do when Mrs. Dillard told her everything?

Nothing seemed to be working out the way Moe had planned. Absolutely nothing.

Late-afternoon sun scorched Moe's neck and shoulders. She cursed the weather. She cursed her sisters. Where were they? It was their fault that Melville had somehow managed to sneak inside Mrs. Dillard's house. Gravel crunched beneath her feet. Bees buzzed. The air was heavy with sweet clover, the sleepy song of birds, and the droning chorus of cicadas.

Moe wiped her sweaty forehead with her sleeve. She passed the biggest, oldest cottonwood in Luck. Hot wind twisted and clattered the tree's heart-shaped leaves together so loudly, the sound reminded Moe of rain on a tin roof.

Rain! If only she could go somewhere cool and wet. She imagined jumping with Otto from the bridge into the middle of the mill pond where the water was too deep to touch bottom. But she did not want to face Otto right now and admit to him what had happened. And she couldn't return home until she found Winnie and Pearl.

"Hello, Moe!" a voice called, startling her. Mr.

Donnelly pulled the reins, but Clem had already come to a stop. The swayback horse had pulled Mr. Donnelly's ice wagon for so many years, he could practically read his owner's mind.

Water drip-drip-dripped from the wagon to the dusty road. The ice, which had been cut in large chunks from the frozen river last winter, was packed in sawdust in Mr. Donnelly's ice house. When he made deliveries, he cut and measured five-pound blocks of ice using a special scale that hung from the back of the wagon. He carried the ice with long, heavy tongs to his customers' back entrances. Some houses in Luck had special little doors made just for ice deliveries. Mr. Donnelly would open the little door and slide the ice inside. Later the ice was stored in the customer's icebox to keep food cool.

"Any rags, any tin scraps today?" Mr. Donnelly asked. In a small town like Luck, he had two jobs. Not only did he sell and deliver ice, he also collected rags and tin, which he traded for cash.

"Not today," Moe said with a shake of her head.

"You look like you're in a world of worry."

"I suppose maybe I am. Can I have a ride?" She hoped Mr. Donnelly would shave a special piece of ice for her. She liked to see how many seconds she could hold the ice in her mouth until her teeth ached.

"There's always room for one more. Tie the goat to the back and hop aboard. Next stop, San Francisco."

Moe tugged Melville to the back of the wagon and discovered four familiar, dirty bare feet sticking out. "Winnie! Pearl! What are you doing?"

Her sisters sucked slivers of ice and swung their legs back and forth as if they hadn't a care in the world. The water dripped down their dirty arms and streaked their dusty legs. "We're hot," Winnie said.

"So we asked Mr. Donnelly for a ride in the ice wagon," Pearl said. "We tied Melville to a tree so he wouldn't escape."

"Well, he did escape. And he did damage to Mrs. Dillard's house that I have to pay for. Thanks to you." Moe gave her little sisters a baleful stare. Why did she have to be so cursed? Everywhere she went, there were her sisters, ruining everything. She couldn't even enjoy a chunk of ice in peace.

"Wasn't our fault," Winnie said, and slurped loudly. "How was we supposed to know Melville would run off?"

Moe sighed. There was no arguing with her stubborn sisters. If she rode in front with Mr. Donnelly, at least she wouldn't have to listen to them. She crawled up into the front seat beside him.

"Giddyap!" he said in a loud voice.

Clem took a step. Then another. He moved, but it was certainly not very fast. Clem knew his route so well, Mr. Donnelly often read the paper while he drove down the street. He kept up on what was happening in the world because one of his customers, Mr. Gardner, regularly gave him week-old Milwaukee newspapers.

"How's the aer-o-planing business?" Mr. Donnelly asked.

"Not so good," Moe admitted.

"I heard that those Wright boys are planning to fly over New York City, right up the Hudson River."

Moe sighed. "I wish I could be there."

"It's a long way to New York. But when I spot the articles, I'll be sure to save them for you. How's that?" Mr. Donnelly said in a cheerful voice.

Reading about Orville and Wilbur Wright wasn't as exciting as actually seeing them fly. For now at least, newspaper articles would have to do.

"Mr. Donnelly," Moe asked, "you ever owe somebody a lot of money?"

Mr. Donnelly scratched his chin. "I owed my

brother for this wagon until I paid him off. That was back in 'eighty-nine, I believe."

"How'd you come up with the money?"

"Took me years of work. I had to take extra jobs here and there. Delivered laundry, worked as a fry cook, dug graves out at the cemetery."

Moe sighed again. She didn't have years and years to save money to pay back Mrs. Dillard. She had only until Mother came home.

"Whoa, Clem!" Mr. Donnelly pulled up on the reins. "What's going on here?"

Along Main Street, a crew of workers with shovels and pickaxes were digging a long ditch right down the middle of the street. To make way for the workers, horses and wagons lined up single file on one side. One of the workers tipped his cap when he saw Mr. Donnelly and Moe. "New sewer line. Town improvement," he said. "How are you doing, Donnelly? I could sure use a cold drink. You ain't got one in back of that wagon, has you?"

Mr. Donnelly laughed. "Sorry, Al. All I've got's ice and two little girls."

Winnie and Pearl giggled. They jumped and came running around to the front of the wagon.

The man named Al lifted up a shining, empty

Brer Rabbit Karo Syrup pail and set it beside the ditch. "I'm powerful thirsty. How old are you gals?"

"Eight, sir," said Winnie.

Pearl gave her sister a shove. "Seven, sir."

The man winked. "You strong enough to run down to the saloon with this bucket and get it filled with beer? I'll pay you a nickel if you'll rush the growler for me. How does that sound?"

A whole nickel! Moe's heart leapt.

"Our mother don't allow us in the saloon," Winnie announced. "She says it's the devil's workshop."

The men laughed so loudly, Winnie turned bright red and hid behind Moe.

Moe scowled, determined not to let a good business deal slip away. "Excuse me, sir," she said. "Seeing as how you're thirsty, maybe we could interest you in ice-cold lemonade."

Al licked his lips. "How much?"

"Three buckets for two nickels," Moe said. "It's fresh and delicious, and you don't need to go anyplace. We'll bring it right to you."

Mr. Donnelly cleared his throat. "Well, Al, you got three youngsters who are willing to slake your thirst for you. You got any more friends with nickels to spend?"

"Sure, sure," Al said. He laughed and signaled to

two other men, who quickly handed over their buckets.

"I'll be on my way," Mr. Donnelly said. "What should I do with the goat, Moe?"

"Would you leave him at Otto's on your way home?"

"Sure, sure," Mr. Donnelly replied, chuckling. "I don't think Melville would be much good in the delivery business."

Moe turned to Winnie and hissed, "Take Pearl home, and get me the sack of lemons from the pantry, a big spoon, a sharp knife, and the bag of sugar. Think you can remember all that?"

Winnie nodded. "Lemons, spoon, knife, sugar. Lemons, spoon, knife, sugar."

"Hurry fast as you can, so Flora doesn't see you," Moe said, "and meet me back at the pump in the park. Now, run!" As soon as her sisters disappeared, Moe gathered the empty buckets. "I'll be back to collect your nickels when I deliver the lemonade, sir," she told the ditch digger.

"We'll be waiting," Al said.

Moe hurried down the street past the tavern. Ordinarily Mother insisted that she and her sisters cross to the other side. Moe paused. A pair of legs emerged beneath the swinging door. The doors squeaked and swung open, and out flooded the damp, cool smell of wet sawdust, stale beer, and cigar smoke. For an instant, Moe glimpsed inside the smoky room that rang with laughter and the tinny sound of a player piano. She took a deep breath and ran the rest of the way to the park.

It seemed to take forever for her sisters to return with the lemonade supplies. What was taking them so long? When they finally appeared, loaded down with bags, Moe immediately set to work. She cut the lemons in half and squeezed them directly into each bucket. "Now add some sugar," she told Pearl, who used the big spoon. Winnie used all her strength to push the water pump handle up and down. Carefully they filled each bucket with water and stirred the lemonade.

"Needs more sugar," Winnie said, wrinkling up her nose as she licked the spoon.

Moe dumped more sugar into each bucket and stirred again. When they agreed the lemonade was perfect, the three girls walked slowly down the block carrying the heavy buckets. "Don't spill," Moe barked over her shoulder at Pearl, who struggled to follow her across the street.

"My dress!" Pearl howled. Her lip trembled as she looked down at the dark spot.

"It's just lemonade," Moe said. "Keep walking."

"Back so soon?" Al asked. He seemed delighted to have his brimming bucket. So did his friends. When the sweaty men threw back their heads and drained all three buckets, their Adam's apples galloped up and down. "Good work," Al said. He wiped his mouth with the back of his grimy hand. "I got three more friends down the line who want lemonade deliveries, too."

For the rest of the afternoon, Moe and her sisters rushed back and forth between the ditch and the pump, careful not to slosh a single drop. The mound of lemon rinds grew, the sugar bag emptied, and Moe's apron pocket bulged with a growing pile of nickels.

The girls worked so hard, Moe did not have time to count their earnings. Pearl complained that she felt dizzy. "Sit under a tree and fan yourself with a branch," Moe said. While her sisters rested, Moe pulled out a sticky handful of coins and counted. Nearly six dollars! Wouldn't Otto be pleased? If the lemons and sugar could be stretched to last a few more buckets, she'd be able to pay Mrs. Dillard the five dollars she owed her. Any other money would be Moe's and her sisters' to keep.

Moe jumped to her feet. "Got to get back to

work. You stay here if you're tired, Pearl and Winnie." Moe collected two more buckets and filled them. She was walking back across the street when she heard a sound that made the hair on the back of her neck stand on end.

"Madeline Genevieve McDonohugh! What do you think you're doing with all our good lemons and every bit of sugar from the pantry?"

Chapter 7

Moe cringed as she watched Mother dash across the street in her best serge traveling suit. Her angry face was bright red under her tilted flowery hat. "I thought you were coming back tomorrow," Moe said helplessly. She tried tucking the pails of lemonade behind her back. No luck.

"What are you doing? Answer me this minute," Mother demanded. Her eyes darted up and down the street.

"Delivering refreshments," Moe mumbled.

"To whom, may I ask?"

"The ditchdiggers. They're paying us—" Before Moe could finish explaining, Mother reached around behind her, grabbed a pail, and dumped the lemonade into the dirt.

"I'm gone scarcely one week, and I come home to find my daughters associating with the lowest beer drinkers in town. What would the women from the Temperance Union say if they saw you wandering up and down the street in this disgraceful way?" Mother wiped her gloved hands with a delicate handkerchief. "I wouldn't be surprised if the next thing they asked you to do was to go to the tavern for them."

"They already did," Moe said in a small voice.

"The nerve of those filthy, deplorable—"

"They're just hot and thirsty," Moe interrupted. "They asked for beer, but we said we could only give them lemonade. That's what we did. We brought them lemonade."

Mother's mouth dropped open. For once she seemed unable to think what to say.

"Hey, where's my drink?" one of the ditchdiggers shouted, waving to Moe from across the street.

Mother took a deep breath. She adjusted her hat. "Where is Flora? I left her in charge. And where are Winnie and Pearl?"

Moe pointed to the tree where she'd left her two sisters. Mother marched to the shade and pulled them to their feet. "You're filthy! Where are your shoes?"

"Mother!" Pearl cried. "You'll never guess how much money we made."

"I can just imagine," Mother said wearily. "Madeline, I want you to give me the money you made until we decide how you plan to repay me for the sugar and lemons you took without asking."

Moe stared at her feet. "I know what I did was wrong, but I was in a hurry. It was such a good business idea, and I needed five dollars to pay back Mrs. Dillard."

"Mrs. Dillard? What has all this to do with that horrid woman?"

Moe bit her lip. "I owe her money because of what happened to her parlor."

Mother's eyes narrowed. She folded her arms in front of herself. "What happened to her parlor?"

"The damage—the ruined fern, the nibbled sofa pillow, the doily that was chewed to bits."

"Madeline!"

"It wasn't my fault," Moe pleaded. "It was that nasty goat. Somehow he got inside her house and—"

"You let a goat"—Mother's face flushed purple—"in Mrs. Dillard's parlor?"

"Hey, give me back my bucket!" one of the ditch-diggers shouted.

"Get home with your sisters at once, Madeline," Mother said between gritted teeth. "We will discuss this later." Using her handkerchief, she delicately picked up the buckets and hurled them into the ditch. *Clang! Clang!*

"Ouch!" the ditchdigger cried.

After breakfast the next day, Mother surprised Moe by placing her hand gently on her shoulder. "Madeline," she said in a quiet voice so that Flora, Winnie, and Pearl couldn't hear her in the next room, "I have been thinking about what happened yesterday—the unfortunate incident with those ditchdiggers."

"Yes?" Moe said nervously.

"I have decided I judged you too harshly."

Moe felt dumbstruck. "You did?"

"After reflection, I cannot tell you how pleased I am that you offered those men lemonade and turned them away from the evil path of drink."

Moe blushed and stared at her feet. She knew she would have delivered beer if her sisters hadn't made everyone laugh.

"I am so touched by your noble action," Mother continued, "that I've decided to tell everyone what you did at the next meeting of the Women's Christian Temperance Union."

Moe looked up, puzzled. Did this mean she could keep the money they had earned?

"You do understand, don't you, that it was wrong to take the lemons and sugar without asking?"

Moe nodded and looked as sorry as she could.

"And you feel penitent about Mrs. Dillard's damaged parlor?"

Moe nodded vigorously.

Mother smiled. "Good. That's what I wanted to hear."

Moe frowned. Had she been tricked?

"I am keeping three dollars for the sugar and lemons. The rest you will present to Mrs. Dillard."

"*All* of it?" Moe protested.

"All of it," Mother said firmly. "Our family has a reputation to maintain in this community. I will not have someone like Mrs. Dillard going around town accusing us of unscrupulous behavior." She kissed Moe on the top of the head and handed her the remaining nickels tied inside an old handkerchief. "You are setting a marvelous, shining example."

Miserably, Moe gave all her earnings to Mrs. Dillard, who did not even bother to thank her for her trouble. As Moe trudged to Otto's laboratory, she did not feel like a marvelous, shining example. She felt more and more discouraged. Only eleven days until the Fourth of July. She and Otto weren't any closer to finishing the airplane. At this rate, they'd never finish.

"Cheer up," Otto said when she told him what had happened. "I have a plan."

"What is it?"

"We'll collect rags and tin for Mr. Donnelly. He'll give us good money, I bet. All we have to do is find enough stuff to make it worthwhile."

"Where are we going to find enough rags and tin cans?"

"Along the railroad tracks is a good place to start. Sometimes crews drop garbage off the cars as they leave town. And then there's the dump."

"The dump? That's two miles outside town. I'm not supposed to go there."

"No one will know. We'll be back before nightfall."

"How are we going to get there and carry everything back before my parents notice I'm gone?"

"Leave that to me," Otto said mysteriously, and winked. "Just meet me here this afternoon at three o'clock. And don't forget a couple empty feed sacks, if you have any."

Moe rushed through the midday supper of fried chicken. She glanced at the grandfather clock as Ella collected the plates. "May I be excused?" she asked desperately.

"Going to that Otto boy's shed again?" Flora said, raising one eyebrow.

Moe squashed her napkin into a ball and slammed it on the table. Mother gave Father a pleading "You-handle-this-please-dear" look.

Father cleared his throat. "Please answer your sister in a civilized manner, Moe."

"Yes, I am going to Otto's," Moe said. "But I'll be back before dark. Now may I leave the table?"

"Can we go with you?" Winnie begged.

"Please?" Pearl asked.

Before Moe could kick her sisters under the table, Mother announced, "I want you little girls to stay home with me this afternoon and practice embroidery. Someone has to keep a closer eye on you. I will not have you running wild in the streets like those Highview children."

Winnie and Pearl looked crestfallen.

Father dabbed his moustache with his napkin. "I think we all survived admirably in your absence, my dear. Everything was under control."

"I'm not so sure about that," Flora said. "A few

of my belongings seem to have disappeared. I can't find my autograph album anywhere. You wouldn't happen to know where it is, would you, Moe?"

Moe knocked her spoon from the table with her elbow. She hoped that no one could hear how loudly her heart was beating as she bent to pick it up. "I haven't seen it," Moe mumbled.

"Flora," Mother said, "you should really be more careful with your belongings."

"I *am* careful," Flora insisted. "I just don't trust some people who happen to live in this house."

"Excuse me," Moe said angelically. As she hurried out the door, she crossed her fingers. Had she hidden the album well enough that Flora would never find it?

"What took you so long?" Otto demanded as soon as he saw her enter the yard. He glanced at his pocket watch, slung the burlap sack over his shoulder, and shut the laboratory door. "We'll have to hurry if we're going to catch the three fifty-seven."

"We're going on a train ride?" Moe asked as she hurried to catch up.

Otto walked quickly through the tall weeds toward the railroad tracks. "We're catching the freight train to Woonsocket."

Excited, Moe hurried to keep up with Otto. "How do we do that?"

"We jump on just past Big Bend, after the train crosses the bridge. The train moves pretty slowly then. I've jumped on plenty of times. We'll ride as far as the dump, jump off, and collect bottles, cans, and rags at the dump and along the tracks on the way back. We'll be home before anyone knows we're gone."

"What about tramps? I heard Father say there are a lot of tramps along the tracks these days. They're homeless and looking for handouts. He said some of them might be dangerous."

Otto scratched the back of his head. "Most of those tent camps are miles from here. I wouldn't worry too much about tramps. Come on!"

Moe imagined leaving town and never coming back. Would she miss her family? Father, yes. Mother and Winnie and Pearl, maybe. But as for Flora, no, she wouldn't miss her. Thinking of Flora made Moe remember something unpleasant. "Otto, Flora asked about the missing album. She acted very suspicious."

"What did you tell her?"

"Nothing."

"I think you should tell her the truth."

Moe frowned. It was easy enough for Otto to give advice. He didn't have to face Flora in person. Suddenly the idea of never coming home appealed to Moe very much.

Moe and Otto followed the railroad track into the forest outside town. The air smelled of pine. In the shadows the air wasn't as hot. Mosquitoes buzzed. Birds sang in the deep, cool shadows, and every once in a while, Moe heard a quick dash and rustle in the underbrush. Was it a deer, raccoon—or wolf? She walked faster along the railroad ties.

Through the trees she saw the railroad bridge at Big Bend, the place where the tracks crossed Devil's Tooth Ravine. The one-track bridge made of hewn timber stretched two hundred feet across a gorge nearly fifty feet deep.

Moe gulped. "What if the train comes while we're crossing?"

"It won't," Otto said. "The train to Woonsocket doesn't come through here for another half hour or more. It's always late. We have plenty of time to get to the other side." Otto stepped rapidly atop the railroad ties, not even pausing as he made his way across the bridge. "Come on!"

Moe took a deep breath. When she stepped on the first tie, she could see down through two of the wooden supports to the endless, dizzying green of Devil's Tooth. What if she fell? What if—

"Come on!" Otto shouted again.

Her heart pounded in her ears. One step, then another. The bridge stretched endlessly. Halfway across, she heard a noise. The track rumbled. She froze.

"Run!" Otto shouted. "Train's coming!"

Chapter 8

Moe slipped, caught her balance. The track shook. She struggled to lift her skinned knees. One foot after the other. Never fast enough. How much farther? Body bent, arms churning.

"Come on!" Otto called from the other side—safe.

Got to get across. Got to move. The shriek of the distant train whistle shot through her like an electric current. She leapt and leapt again. Five more railroad ties to the end of the bridge. Metal shimmied. Behind her—how far?—the steady rumble bearing down, closer, closer.

"You can make it!" Otto shouted.

Three ties—two—then one. She jumped off the track into the tall weeds. She rolled on solid ground, stopped, and sat up gulping for air. Her throat burned. Her chest ached.

The big black engine burst into sight. The whistle pierced the air again. The engine slowed, sending a hollow, ringing noise through the rails and across the bridge's timbers.

"Get up!"

Moe felt Otto pulling her arm, hoisting her to her feet once the engine roared past. The ground rolled and buckled. Now train cars—hundreds of them – lumbered by in a dizzying, endless parade. Moe's hair whipped her face. Dust blew. The great, gray, heavy wheels sang and clattered. *How close. How enormous.* She stared, numb. "I could still be out there," she said. But her voice could not be heard above the deafening noise.

"There's an open car!" Otto shouted. Moe felt her legs move. She was running again. Otto was pulling her. "Don't look down!" he called. "Keep your eyes on the door!"

She stumbled along the rocky embankment. But Otto did not let go of her hand until he reached the open door. He threw the burlap sacks into the slow-moving train car and grabbed the iron bar handle beside the door. He leapt and thrust one foot onto the lowest rung of a metal ladder that hung beneath the door. Expertly he scrambled inside the train car. On his knees, he extended his hand to Moe, who kept running alongside. "Come on!"

"I can't!" she screamed. Her feet felt as heavy as anvils. Her legs ached. How much longer could she keep running?

"You don't want to be left behind, do you?" he called. "Come on!"

The dark forest. Wolves. Tramps, maybe. She had to reach his hand and get into that train car, no matter what. She grabbed and missed.

"You can do it!" he shouted as the train began to pick up speed.

She reached again. He snatched her hand and held tight. With her other hand, she gripped the bar. Otto pulled her up. She managed to swing one foot inside the ladder rung.

"Swing your other leg up. That's it," he said, and dragged her inside. She flopped on the floor like a hooked fish. With her cheek pressed to the straw-littered floor, she tried to catch her breath. She closed her eyes. The swaying train clanked and clinked over the tracks as soothing as a lullaby.

"When we get to the dump," Otto said, "we jump off."

Moe lifted her head and stared at Otto in disbelief. "Jump?"

"That's right. Otherwise we'll end up all the way to Chaffee City. That's a long walk back."

She sat up. If she had had the energy, she would have punched that carefree smile off his face. "How do you jump off a moving train?"

"It's easy. Just watch what I do when the time comes," he said. "Then we wander to the dump, collect as much as we can, and follow the tracks back to town."

"All the way back to Luck?" Moe felt overwhelmed by a sinking feeling. Whom might they meet miles and miles through the dark woods?

"What's the matter? You scared?"

Moe shook her head. She wouldn't give Otto the satisfaction of knowing how terrified she really felt. Gazing through the open doorway, she watched trees roll past. A deer darted across a clearing. Swallows somersaulted in midair. Whose bright eyes were those staring out from under a bush?

Moe glanced around the train car, which smelled of straw and dust. In a corner were a few torn scraps of cardboard, maybe some other traveler's mattress. Lying down on the floor, she cradled her head in one elbow and closed her eyes. The rhythm of the train lulled her to sleep.

"Wake up!" Otto shouted. "We've got to jump. We're almost to the dump."

Moe rubbed her eyes. She looked out the open door. Now the shadows had become longer, blacker. How far had they traveled?

Otto crouched in the doorway with the sacks in one hand, watching the ground. "The train's slowing down again. You go first. Look for a grassy place, and land on your feet."

A breeze blew Moe's hair every which way. She tried to study the ground, but everything seemed a dizzy blur. Just when she was about to jump, she looked back at Otto. For the first time, she saw terror on his face. His big eyes bulged out, and his face went pale.

"What's wrong?" she shouted.

He didn't answer. Instead he tilted his head toward his hand, clenched to the bar. What was it? Moe looked.

An enormous spider.

The spider crawled slowly down the inside of the door toward Otto's white-knuckled fist.

"Let go, Otto. Come over to this side. The spider

won't bother you," Moe said. She pulled on his elbow.

Otto wouldn't budge. He seemed frozen to that bar, holding fast for dear life. The spider crawled closer.

"We'll be miles past the dump. We've got to jump," Moe urged.

Otto refused to move, refused to speak. He bit his lip and kept watching the spider. What should she do? Moe tried to pry his hand free, but it was clutched tight. She pulled on one arm. No good.

In desperation she hurried to the dark corner of the train car and came back with a piece of cardboard. Using the cardboard like a scoop, she brushed the spider from the wall and hurled the piece of cardboard out the door.

"It's gone, Otto. Now you can let go."

Otto's jaw twitched. "Are ... are you sure?"

Moe nodded. Ordinarily Otto was one of the bravest people she knew. Why did something as small as a spider scare him so badly? It was a mystery to her. But since he was her friend, she didn't torment him by asking. She just let it be.

Otto unhinged his fingers from the bar. Moe tucked the burlap sacks under her arm.

"Ready?" she shouted, grabbing his hand.

"One—two—three—jump!" They flew through the air and landed on a grassy incline. Moe let go of Otto and rolled.

Otto stood up and brushed himself off. He picked up the burlap sacks. "See?" he said, his old confidence returning. "That wasn't so hard, was it?"

Moe rubbed her sore elbow, which poked through the rip in her dress sleeve. "You know where we are?"

Otto scanned the surrounding trees. "I thought the dump was somewhere around here. But in the dark it's hard to tell."

Moe shivered. For the first time, she wished she were home again. "What are we going to do?"

"Walk along the tracks the same way we came. We won't get lost." Otto hoisted the sacks to his shoulder and started trudging between the rails. *Clang!* "Found a tin can," he said triumphantly, and put the can in the bag. "One of those rich railroad workers must have thrown it from the train."

Moe didn't say anything, but she felt very uneasy. They had no candle, no lantern. What if the forest became so dark they couldn't see where they were walking? To keep up her courage, she concentrated on the track ahead and searched for cans. Sometimes she sang songs like "Darling Clementine" and

"I've Been Working on the Railroad," and Otto joined in on the chorus. After more than an hour of walking, neither of them recognized any familiar landmark.

Otto stopped abruptly and grabbed Moe's arm. From somewhere deep in the forest came a high, mournful howling. Moe felt as if her heart was beating inside her mouth.

"What's that?" she whispered.

"Coyotes, most likely," Otto replied. "Let's keep moving."

Moe and Otto stopped looking for cans. They stopped singing and telling jokes. Instead they moved as fast as they could. Her stomach growled, adding to her misery. By now she knew her mother had probably noticed she was missing. Moe wished she'd left behind a note saying where she'd gone. What if something happened to her? No one would even know where to look for her.

"What's up ahead?" Otto whispered. "I think I see a light."

Moe gulped. "A train?"

"There's no train that passes this way so late."

"You think it's tramps?"

Otto cleared his throat. His voice sounded as if he was struggling very hard to be calm. "I bet it's the ghost of a train. I heard about that Number Fifty-seven Mr. Donnelly likes to tell about. You know, the one that crashed years ago, but they still see the lantern light come through across the field and down the track."

"Shut up," Moe hissed. "Stop trying to scare me."

"Make a lot of noise so they can hear us coming." He kicked rocks so they clanged against the track.

"Maybe it's somebody out walking just like us." She didn't want to say what she was really thinking. What if the person up ahead was a no-good stranger? Maybe some kind of crazy tramp or a criminal escaped from the county prison?

As Moe and Otto came closer, the light bobbed off into the woods. For an instant, it seemed to disappear.

"Maybe they're waiting to ambush us," Moe said, her voice trembling. "Maybe they're hiding, waiting for us to pass, and then they're going to jump out and—"

Otto grabbed Moe's arm. "Run!"

They both ran. Moe ran faster than she ever had in her life. She raced down the track, past the spot where the light had disappeared. From the woods came the sound of laughter—or the hooting of an owl? Moe didn't slow down. She kept running, cans clanging and banging, terrified to look back.

When they reached the ravine, they decided the safest way to cross the bridge was on their hands and knees. "We'll just have to feel each railroad tie as we go," Otto said.

Moe was glad there wasn't a moon. Then she'd be able to see down into the bottom of the ravine. "You're sure there's no train?"

"I'm sure," Otto replied.

As she crossed, Moe heard a muffled crash in the trees below them. She froze. "Otto?" she said in a little voice.

"I'm all right. But I dropped the bag of cans."

By the time they reached Luck, it was nearly eleven o'clock, according to the clock on the village hall tower. Fireflies darted across the bushes. Moe thought she'd never seen anything so beautiful as the light in her house's kitchen window. She left Otto and slunk to the back door, hoping somehow to slip inside without anyone noticing.

The screen door squeaked. "Madeline Genevieve McDonohugh?" Mother called shrilly from the parlor. "Is that you?"

Moe slumped against the kitchen wall. She knew her life would soon be over.

Chapter 9

Mother did not look kindly upon Moe's explanation of her freight train ride. "That was a very dangerous thing to do," Mother said. "Your punishment for the next four days will be work. You will help with inventory at the store, where Father can keep an eye on you so that you stay out of trouble."

Moe did not know what was worse, not seeing Otto for four days or performing the boring task of counting cans of potted ham, boxes of oatmeal, and pails of quince jelly.

"Chin up," Father said the next morning with a wink. "You can help me with the new soda fountain. Come along now, or we'll be late for work."

Moe smiled halfheartedly and followed Father out the front door. Only ten days until the Fourth of

July. And if she could not see or speak with Otto during that time, how would they ever finish the airplane?

Moe and Father passed the blacksmith's shop. She sniffed the early-morning air and smelled coal smoke from the smithy's fire, which never went out, even on the hottest days. *Clang! Clang! Clang!* The blacksmith's heavy hammer rang out. Loafers sat on a bench in the shade beside the smithy's door and spat tobacco juice into the dust. Father waved hello. The old men waved back.

Moe sniffed the air again as they passed another shop. This time she caught a whiff of bread baking, sauerkraut stew, and—what was that other smell? Maybe green coffee beans roasting in a big black fry kettle.

"Come on, Moe," Father called.

Moe hurried to catch up. Dogs barked near the confectionery shop. Two sheep behind the milliner's store butted up against the wooden slats of a fence. Flies buzzed. Children shouted from behind the Buena Vista House. A hoop flew past.

"Where you going in such a hurry?" Father called to a galloping barefoot boy.

The boy waved and kept running after the hoop. Moe watched him disappear into the alley, wishing she could run barefoot and free today, too. She dug her boot heels into the wagon-wheel paths of soft dirt, being careful to tiptoe around piles of fly-specked horse manure and not to breathe through her nose. A wagon rolled slowly past. Its steel-rimmed wheels made a high grinding noise as they bit the ground.

"Going to be another scorcher." Father paused and wiped his forehead with a handkerchief. In spite of the heat, he wore his usual suit: a dark buttoned coat and a stiff linen collar. When he arrived at the store, Moe knew he would remove his coat and put on a long white apron. Mother didn't like to see Father in shirtsleeves. "It's disgraceful in public," she always said. "You look like a clerk."

"I *was* a clerk before I married you," was Father's usual reply.

Father unlocked the store, which had been founded by Grandpa Humphery, Mother's father. Moe stood in the semidarkness of the doorway and decided that this was how heaven must look and smell—everything new and shining and mysteriously fragrant and hopeful.

Red, yellow, and green wool blankets hung from the ceiling bright as flags. Shovels with gleaming faces lined up above never-been-used manure forks and pitchforks. Bolts of fabric stood side by side: turkey red and the dull black sateen of mourning cloth beside flowered flannel and polka-dot dimity. Slanting rays of sunlight through the big front window glinted against green glass Mason jars, hurricane lamp globes, and small glass bottles of Rex Kidney and Liver Bitters and Pure Sweet Oil, a remedy for ear infections.

Moe ran her hand over the glass counter that protected shining thimbles and folding pocketknives, gold-plated watch fobs and women's pins, and expensive white carved pipes. Near the big cash box was the five-and-ten-cent counter—an array of inexpensive, tempting items that included everything from crochet hooks, wash basins, and baby bibs to watch keeps and harmonicas.

In another display along the wall, ribbons curled around paper cylinders like tight fists. Above the ribbons hung dazzling washboards, an army of scrub brushes, and boxes of Pear's lilac-scented soap. The store was crowded with smells—fresh apples, pungent dill pickles, tobacco plugs, mummified chunks of dried codfish. And from huge hogshead barrels, sweet black molasses dripped fragrantly through a bunghole into a bucket.

Father's latest pride and joy was the soda fountain. Mother preferred to call it a "Temperance Bar," because no liquor was served. The long, shining mahogany counter stretched along one side of the store. Tucked up against the counter were high-backed wire chairs. Behind the counter was an ice box that held three flavors of ice cream: chocolate, strawberry, and vanilla. Above the counter were three elegant silver spigots. One squirted strawberry syrup, the other chocolate, and the last produced fizzy carbonated water, guaranteed to cure "constipation, indigestion, and obesity."

Father, burly and stoop-shouldered, looked very thoughtful as he filled tall glasses of fizzy water. He spent hours experimenting with extracts of lemon, ginger, and sarsaparilla to concoct all kinds of new sweet soda-water drinks. "Nothing successful yet, but I expect a breakthrough any moment," he boasted to his many friends, who had one more reason to linger at the store and sample his latest creation. When he wasn't creating a new soda treat, he took great pride in polishing the soda fountain's gleaming mirror, which had come all the way from Chicago, and rearranging the bright galloping-cowboy chromo prints sent by the insurance company.

Humphery's Dry Goods not only had the first

soda fountain in town, it also had the first telephone. The remarkable telephone hung on the wall, a wooden box with a long cord attached to a black, cone-shaped listening device. "Grandpa Humphery always said that stores sell by example," Mother had announced when the telephone was installed. Moe enjoyed the telephone, too, but for reasons that had nothing to do with improving sales.

"Moe, my dear, you are being drafted to dust," Father said. "Tomorrow we'll begin inventory as your mother requested. Although I prefer not to know what we have not sold, your mother seems to find the numbers particularly fascinating." He took off his coat and slipped his apron over his head. He handed Moe a smaller version of the same apron and a feather duster.

Moe dusted the pyramid of five-cent packages of Uneeda Biscuits in airtight patented moisture-proof wrappers. She dusted the poster of the boy in the yellow storm slicker that said: "Lest you forget, we say it yet. Uneeda Biscuit."

Looking at the boy in the rain slicker made her think of Otto. What was he doing? She hoped he was working on the airplane model. Perhaps he would wonder why she didn't come to the laboratory. Perhaps he would come to the store trying to find her. But Otto never came. At five o'clock it was time to go home.

The next day Moe counted cans of asparagus, peaches, and apricots. She arranged bolts of cloth by color. By eleven o'clock in the morning, she was hot and bored and wished she could go swimming in the mill pond. She stared at the telephone and considered picking up the receiver. But Father did not approve of her listening in on other people's conversations. Moe sighed. Where was Otto? She hoped he wasn't out having fun while she was trapped indoors doing dull chores. After all, it had been *his* idea to hitch a ride on the freight train. And now she was in trouble. This did not seem the least bit fair.

"Really, Moe, must you whack the wool blankets so hard?" Father called to her through the open doorway.

"Sorry," Moe said. She folded the blankets carefully, carried them inside, and placed them on the shelf. "Nobody wants blankets in the summertime."

"You seem in a terrible humor this morning."

"I'm not," Moe said vehemently. "I'm perfectly fine."

Father shrugged and retreated behind the soda fountain bar.

"Do you have any paper I might use?" she asked. "I'd like to write a note."

"If it will cheer you up, help yourself. There's paper on the desk in the back room."

Moe opened the drawer and took out a piece of paper and a fountain pen. "Father, have you any vinegar I could use?"

"Check the barrel," Father said. He was busy mixing a glass of soda water and cranberry juice for a customer.

Moe dipped the fountain pen in vinegar, which she had poured into a small cup. She wrote:

Dear Otto:
Please come and see me TODAY. I am trapped in the store.

—Moe

She blew on the invisible ink handwriting, which Otto himself had taught her how to make. He was so clever sometimes. All he'd have to do when he received the letter was hold it up in front of a candle. Then the words would appear. But how would she deliver the letter if she couldn't leave the store? Moe folded the page in half and tucked it inside an envelope. She wrote "Price Evans Furniture and Undertaking—Otto—Secret" on the envelope.

"Father," she asked in her most polite voice, "will you please drop off a letter for me at Price Furniture on your way to the Lodge meeting today?"

"Certainly, my dear."

While her father was busy that afternoon serving as Most Illustrious Grand Potentate at his Lodge meeting, Moe waited. An hour crawled past, but there was no visit from Otto, no hand-delivered invisible secret answer to her letter. She looked at the clock. Two more hours until closing, and still no Otto. Where was he? Moe paced the store, swiping at the counter with a feather duster. How could he desert her like this? What a scoundrel! He wasn't her friend at all.

She smacked the broom against the floor. When she picked it up, she noticed the telephone's two bright bells staring down at her like friendly eyes. She went closer and reached as high as she could, but she couldn't touch the hand crank on the side of the walnut case. On the other side was the tempting receiver, which hung from a wire on a hook.

Stealthily she pushed a chair next to the telephone. She climbed up and lifted the receiver as quietly as possible so that no one talking could hear her. Putting the receiver to her ear, she listened. The line clicked. "Hello, Central?"

Moe recognized the demanding, high-pitched voice immediately. It was Mrs. Critchfield ringing up the operator, whose name was Alvira Johnson. Everyone called her Alphie. Alphie's switchboard, the only one in town, was located in the millinery shop down the street. To call another telephone number, it was necessary first to ring up Alphie, who made the connection. Even though everyone knew Alphie was the operator, callers still said, "Hello, Central." Moe did not understand why.

"It's Blanche. Ring me up in fifteen minutes, so that I won't forget to take the bread out of the oven."

"Sure thing, Blanche." *Click.*

Moe scowled. Nothing interesting about bread rising. She waited.

"Hello, Central?"

"May I help you?"

"Give me Belle Eastman."

Moe licked her lips. She glanced toward the door, hoping Father wouldn't walk in and ruin everything. Mrs. Eastman was one of the most tireless and accomplished gossips in Luck.

"Hello, Belle."

"Willamena dear? Did you hear that the Price boy is back? Word is that he's going to college in the fall."

"You don't say."

"And he had an offer to work at the meat-packing plant in Milwaukee. But did he do good by his father and earn money? No. He's going to college. Such a waste! Did you ever hear of anything more useless?"

"*Tsk-tsk.*"

"He's spent the last two days since he's been home at the swimming hole when he should be making money for school. That whole wild bunch. Up to no good. And even his forlorn brother. You know the child I mean? The skinny one. Doesn't look a lick like his brother or father. Right after he was born, of course, that's when she left for good."

"Who?"

"You know who I mean. His mother. I don't think it's a good idea for a young boy to hang around those older rascals who don't do anything all day but hang out at the pool hall and swim in the mill pond. I wouldn't be surprised if they smoked behind the mill. I smelled something when I was down that way."

"You don't say?"

"You know I'm not one to gossip, but that's what I suspect. Those Price boys don't have a lick of sense. Just look what happened to their mother—"

Click. Moe slammed down the receiver. Swimming in the mill pond with his brother and his friends! So that's where Otto had been all this time. No wonder he didn't have time to find out what had happened to her.

What was even worse was that when Otto's brother and his friends took over the mill pond, girls weren't allowed. That was because the bossy boys refused to wear bathing suits. It was so unfair. The only decent place to swim had suddenly become off limits. Well, she'd show traitorous Otto and his hearts-and-kisses brother. She'd teach them both a lesson they'd never forget.

Chapter 10

After supper that night, Moe secretly made her way to the mill pond. If she were caught by her parents, she knew she would be in terrible trouble. But she didn't care. She was on an important mission. Even before she arrived at the trees lining the muddy bank of the mill pond, she heard the sounds of laughter and splashing in the evening shadows.

"Jump, Otto!"

"I will when I'm ready."

Moe recognized Otto's voice and that of his older brother. There were other voices as well—cousins, friends from town, the wild fellows Otto's brother met with regularly at the pool hall.

Mosquitoes buzzed around Moe's face. She felt hot and miserable. While she had been slaving away in Father's store, Otto and his brother and his friends were enjoying themselves. And in two more days, when she was finally free, she wouldn't be allowed to join them at the swimming hole because she was a girl.

It wasn't fair.

She slipped off her shoes and waded upstream through the creek that emptied into the mill pond. The summer heat and no rain for weeks had dried the edges of the creek bed so that mud lay in cracked ridges that looked like half-buried ribs. As she walked, the water became shallower and shallower. When she glanced down at her ankles, she saw crabs scurry desperately below the surface. She pushed a long stick into the water, and the crabs clamped tightly to the end of it with their pinchers. She threw a pebble. The crabs darted and crashed into each other. *Splash!*

"Can't catch me!" the boys shouted upstream.

Moe smiled. The crabs had given her an idea. Inspired, she hurried through the semidarkness back to the house. Her plan would not fail.

After a very dull morning and afternoon the next day counting sticky rubber-coated galoshes, umbrellas, and rain hats that no one wanted to buy, Moe was eager to return home. She finished her supper quickly and slipped outside to the garden shed. There she found exactly what she was looking for— a big bucket with a handle. She hoped she wasn't too late as she ran to the creek, swinging the bucket.

The sun was beginning to disappear behind the trees. Birds flapped and dunked their heads in the shallow water. Moe tipped the bucket into a low pool. She used a stick to scoop up crabs. The eager creatures scrambled into the bucket, which was half filled with water. Their claws and hard bodies made scratching noises against the bucket's metal sides. When she'd filled it with crabs, she hoisted the heavy, sloshing bucket with both hands and headed to the mill pond.

Carefully she tipped the bucket in the best swimming spot, near an overhanging tree. The crabs scurried over each other in their rush for deep water. They landed *plop-plop-plip*. "Good luck," Moe whispered. She plunged into the bushes and hid just in time. Coming through the woods with loud, boastful shouts were Otto, his brother, and his friends.

They stripped off their clothing and hung their pants and shirts on bushes, not realizing, of course, that Moe hid nearby. The swimmers scurried out of sight, around to the overhanging tree, which was used as a diving board. As soon as their backs were turned, Moe stealthily gathered all their clothing in a big pile and ran as fast as she could. The empty metal pail bumped against her legs, but Moe did not care. When she reached the well near the abandoned orchard, she stuffed the clothing down.

Moe took the long way home and arrived back at the garden shed and replaced the bucket before Mother noticed she was gone. To complete her angelic image, she climbed the stairs with the latest issue of *Godey's Ladies Book* under her arm to read before she went to sleep.

The next day, Moe's last in the store, she tried to be especially helpful. She dusted the fishing rods and shined the genuine silver-plated teapots. She wiped the soda fountain bar spigots until they sparkled, and she rearranged the soda glasses. But she could not help wondering what had happened last night at the mill pond. Had the crabs done their job?

Unable to stand the uncertainty another moment, she picked up the telephone receiver while Father argued politics outside with Mr. Simpson.

"... So I says, 'How should I know?' And then he says, 'Because it's your job.' So I says ..."

Moe hung up, disappointed that the talk wasn't about Ben, Otto, and the other swimmers. She pushed the broom across the floor again.

"Delivery, Moe!" Father announced through the open door. "It's the fruit I've been expecting from Milwaukee. Something special. Wait until you see." Father hurried out to the boardwalk, where a horse and wagon had arrived from the train station. He helped the driver haul inside a large wooden crate painted with the word "Produce."

"What's in there?" Moe asked.

Father paid the driver and rummaged in the back room for a crowbar. He struggled for several moments prying open the crate. "Look what came thousands and thousands of miles from the jungles of South America!"

Moe rushed to take a look. But when she peered inside the crate, she discovered a disappointing green and spindly clump. "What is it?"

"Fresh bananas all the way from South America."

Moe slid her finger across one of the long, green fruits. The skin seemed leathery and tough. Somehow bananas did not look the least bit fascinating or appetizing.

"When they ripen, they'll turn bright yellow," Father said. "I need to put an ad in the newspaper as soon as possible to announce their arrival. We don't want to lose money on this expensive South American venture, or we'll never hear the end of it from your mother." Father took his hat from the hook behind the door. "While I'm gone, make a sign, will you, and put it in the window? 'Freshest Bananas from South America.' Should be a sensation."

Moe didn't think there was anything sensational about green, spindly fruit, but she did as she was told. She found a piece of brown butcher paper and a black grease pencil Father used to mark prices on the backs of china cups and plates. How was she supposed to make a sign when she didn't know how to spell the name of the fruit? She wished she hadn't forgotten to ask Father before he left. She couldn't leave the store unattended while she ran home to ask Mother. What should she do?

Moe pushed a chair to the wall and stood on it. She rang the telephone and cleared her throat. "Hello, Central?"

"Yes?"

"This is Moe down at Humphery's. You know how to spell *banana?*"

There was a long pause. "Let me think. I'll take

a wild guess. B-A-N-N-A-N-N-A. You got some down at the store?"

"Yes," Moe said. "B-A-N-N-A-N-N-A. Tell everybody you talk to, will you? Father's worried the fruit will rot before he can sell it."

"Sure thing. And tell your father to save a soda for me, will you, Moe? I'm awful parched."

"Good-bye." Moe hung up the phone and repeated the spelling so she wouldn't forget. B-A-N-N-A-N-N-A. She hopped off the chair and felt very proud. Her first phone call! And she had not had to ask any grown-up for help. Carefully she wrote "BANNANNA" in big letters on a piece of brown paper and taped the sign inside the window. As soon as she finished, she saw a familiar shape shuffling down the boardwalk toward the store.

"Hello, Moe," said Otto, coming through the front door. He had a sheepish look on his face. His cheeks were sunburned, and his hair was combed, for once.

"Hello yourself," Moe replied gruffly.

"You spelled *banana* wrong."

Moe glared at Otto. She wondered if he'd come all this way just to torment her for her bad spelling. But all she said was, "I hear your brother's back in town."

Otto nodded. "He leaves today for a threshing crew in Iowa."

"What do you have to say for yourself?" she demanded.

Otto looked bewildered. "Nothing."

"Aren't you going to say 'sorry'?"

"Why?"

Moe let out a big mouthful of air. "For not coming here when I wrote to you. For not answering my note. That was rude. Of course, you were so busy swimming, you probably didn't have time to read your mail."

"What mail?"

"The message in the envelope I sent to you three days ago. Father said he delivered it."

Otto screwed up his mouth as if he were deep in thought. "Didn't get any message."

"I sent it the regular way. Invisible ink."

Otto smiled. "So *that's* what that was. I got an envelope with a piece of paper inside that looked blank. I never thought it was—well, sorry, Moe. I didn't think it was from you."

"Who'd you think it was from?" Moe looked away so that he couldn't see the hurt expression on her face. "All this time I've been trapped here. Four days. Mother said it was my punishment for going on the freight train with you. I bet your father didn't even care you disappeared."

Otto shrugged. "Can't say he noticed," he said in a small voice. "I'm sorry you got into trouble. I didn't know. I thought you were just mad at me, that's why you weren't coming to the laboratory. So I went off with my brother and his friends."

Moe snorted. "Swimming, right?"

"Until yesterday." Otto rubbed his backside. "Don't think we'll go tonight. Strangest thing happened last night. Right when we jumped into the swimming hole, we were attacked by these crabs. Don't remember ever seeing crabs in the swimming hole before. They latched on to us and wouldn't let go. When we pried some of them loose and managed to wade to shore, wouldn't you know it but our clothes were gone!

"My brother and his friends were mad as anything. Vowed they'd never swim there again. We had to get back to our houses somehow. So we grabbed some branches."

Moe turned away quickly so that Otto couldn't see how hard she was laughing.

"What's so funny? Hey, Moe, did you know about this?" Otto demanded. "I have a feeling you had something to do with those crabs."

"I did," Moe blurted. She bent over and laughed so hard, tears came to her eyes.

"It was a mean trick."

Moe wiped her eyes with her apron. "I'm sorry. I guess I thought you'd deserted me. I thought you'd given up on the airplane, too."

"I don't give up that easily," Otto said with a smile.

Moe grinned. It felt good to be friends again. She could hardly wait to get back to work on the airplane. "I want to show you something," Moe said eagerly. "Father had a delivery that came in a big wooden crate. Maybe he'll let us have the wood when he gets done prying it apart. Let me show you."

Moe led Otto to the back of the store, where the bananas were still crated. Suddenly Otto froze. He did not speak. He extended one finger and pointed to the ground. What was wrong?

"Come on, Otto," Moe said. "It's just bananas. Nothing to be scared of."

But when she looked where he was pointing, she saw the biggest, hairiest spider she had ever seen.

The giant brown spider crept slowly toward them across the floorboards. It looked almost six inches wide—as big as Moe's outstretched hand. The creature paused as if to consider its surroundings. Moe watched, fascinated. But when she looked at Otto, she noticed that his face had changed to pale green.

"Don't worry, Otto," she said quietly. "I'm sure it won't hurt us." She tiptoed to the nearby bargain counter and grabbed a thirty-cent genuine pressed-glass berry dish. She crept across the floor, past quivering Otto, and circled slowly. The spider reared up on its back legs and made a threatening noise that sounded like a low purr. Moe clamped the berry dish upside-down over the spider.

Otto's knees buckled. He fell to the floor with a clunk.

Before Moe could move to help him, Father returned. "What's Otto doing passed out on the floor?" he said. He lifted Otto's head and patted his cheek. "Get the smelling salts from the medicine display. Next to the cod liver oil, I think."

Moe did as she was told. Father held the vial of ammonia spirits under Otto's nose. Otto moved his head. His eyelids fluttered, and he sneezed. "I think you'll be all right now, old chap," Father said. Looking curiously at Moe, he asked, "What made him keel over?"

"That," said Moe, pointing to the upside-down berry dish.

Father crept closer for a better look. Now Father's face turned pale green. "Oh, my—"

"What is it?" Moe demanded.

"Tarantula!" Father rasped.

Chapter 11

"The spider must have been hiding in the banana crate," Father whispered nervously. "We can't let him go. He might bite someone."

"I found him, and I refuse to let him be killed," Moe announced in an indignant voice. "He's come thousands and thousands of miles to get here. It wouldn't be fair to destroy him now. And think of it! There's never been anything this exotic in Luck, Wisconsin."

Father did not look convinced. He kept his distance.

"What if we keep him trapped so he'll never escape?" Moe said. "I'll make sure he doesn't run off." The spider scrambled upside-down along the glass. His black eyes stared out at her. "Are you sure he's poisonous?"

"I've heard people say that one bite from a tarantula can cause terrible melancholy," Father said, pacing back and forth. "The only way to rid yourself of the deadly poison is to dance."

"Dance?" Moe looked closely at the tarantula with even more respect. For the first time, she noticed that the underside of each leg tip had a pad of iridescent hairs. Magic spider dancing shoes.

Otto sat up and rubbed his head. "Dancing doesn't sound like a very scientific cure to me. I think we need to go to the library and search out something on South American spiders. How else are we going to know what to feed it?"

"I thought you hated spiders," Moe said.

"I do." Otto stood up and brushed himself off. He walked toward the berry bowl—not too close, just a few feet away. He squinted down at the hairy creature. "I can't let it starve, even if it is a spider."

"Good man," Father said. "Now I've got some important work to do in the store. I suggest moving the spider from the middle of the floor before it scares away every single customer." He looked at Moe. So did Otto. It was clear the job of finding a secure home for the spider was going to be hers.

While Otto went off to the library, Moe searched the store for stiff packing cardboard. She slid the cardboard under the overturned berry dish. The muscular spider did not seem pleased but jumped onto the cardboard so that Moe could carefully turn it over and prevent him from escaping. "Sorry," she said.

"Now secure the edges of the cardboard to the dish with this packing tape. Use plenty," Father said, refusing to come any closer than he had to. "And make sure you punch some holes so the spider can breathe."

Thanks to the operator, Alphie, who talked to the librarian, almost everyone in Luck soon found out that there was a captive, man-eating spider from South America in Humphery's Dry Goods. By the time Otto returned from the library, a small crowd of grown-ups and children had lined up outside the store doorway. Everyone was talking at once.

"It bite anyone yet?"

"I say we blast the monster's head off."

"No need to panic," Father announced, smiling. "Everything's completely under control. This young man's a spider expert. He can tell us all about the tarantula, can't you, Otto?"

Otto blushed. "It's actually a hairy Mygalomorph."

"Can't hear a word," someone called. "Stand on the bench and speak up, will you?"

Otto cleared his throat. He stepped up onto the bench outside the door. "The phylum is *Arthropoda,* the class *Arachnida,* and the order *Araneae.* I'm not sure, but I think it might be a bird-eating spider."

"What the blazes is that?"

"You mean it attacks chickens?"

"No," Otto said. "In the tropical jungles in South America, the spider only comes out at night to hunt hummingbirds, small snakes, maybe reptiles. During the day, it hides in cracks in rocks or holes in trees. When the spider's ready to attack its prey, it runs it down and seizes it in a sudden, silent dash."

"Sounds sneaky to me."

"Whoever heard of a bug that can carry off snakes? How big's this thing, anyhow?"

One of the women from Mother's Sunshine Bible Group pushed her way to the front of the crowd. "Does the sheriff know you're keeping this creature here, Mr. McDonohugh?"

Father shook his head. "Now, there's no need to worry. This spider is safely locked up where it won't bother anyone." He motioned to Moe and Otto and said to them in a low voice, "You're going to need to find a new home for the spider outside the store. He's making folks too nervous."

Moe glanced at the crowd. They reminded her of

the people who came to Norman Dubie's field to watch heroic Art Taylor sail through the sky. Moe smiled. Maybe something wonderful might come of this tarantula after all.

"Father," she said, "can I take the spider out back and keep him behind a fence where no one can touch him?"

Father wiped his sweaty forehead with his handkerchief. "Yes, yes. Just get him out of the store. Everyone's afraid to come in. Your mother will have a fit if she finds out how we're losing business."

"Come with me, Otto," Moe said. She hurried into the back room of the store and found a large piece of brown wrapping paper. "We're going to make a sign. You write it, since you know how to spell." She handed Otto a black crayon. "Write 'Killer Spider from South America, 5 Cents.' "

Otto frowned.

"Write it."

For once, Otto did as Moe said. She tacked their sign on the wall outside the store. While Otto drew an arrow pointing around toward the yard behind the building, Moe carefully carried the tarantula in its bowl out back and set it on an old table. She unrolled chicken wire Father had left under the back steps and made a rude fence around the table.

Then she hung an old canvas tarp from the clothes-
line which extended from the store to a pole,
shielding the tarantula on the table from view.

"Are you ready?" Otto hissed. He peered around
the corner of the store. "They're all waiting in line."

"Come one! Come all!" Moe shouted in her best
Medicine Show hawker voice.

Otto collected money as grown-ups and children
pushed and shoved around the store. They craned
their necks for a better look after hearing about the
infamous creature that had become the talk of the
whole town. Even Ben Price and his friends came.
Flora appeared briefly, looking longingly at Otto's
brother. Ben did not bother to talk to or even look
at her.

When Moe saw Flora's sad expression, she offered to let her see the spider a second time for
free—just to cheer her up.

"Why should I want to view a vile insect again?"
Flora said angrily, and stomped away.

Moe shook her head. She wondered if she would
ever understand her sister.

All day long, people filed past the spider and
peered into the berry dish. Many people came four
or five times. Otto's pockets were soon so full of

money, he had to use an old pillowcase to store the coins.

"Otto, tell how the spider eats," Pearl said with a rapt expression. Moe's younger sisters had showed up with Flora and never left Otto's side.

Otto looked irritated. "I already told it a dozen times."

"Tell it again," Pearl begged. She nudged Winnie.

"Please?" Winnie whined.

Otto took a deep breath. "The spider catches hummingbirds, drags them from their nests, and stabs them with sharply pointed hollow fangs."

One girl in the crowd screamed.

"Tell the rest," Pearl said. "You didn't finish."

"Then the spider injects fluid. This powerful juice helps the spider digest its prey, because it liquefies the inside of the victim's body before the spider sucks out the contents."

Even the boys looked impressed. One little girl started sobbing.

Pearl smiled at the crowd. "See, I told you it was exciting."

For the next three days, Moe and Otto managed to collect twenty-three dollars and seventy-six cents from admission to see the spider.

"This is the most money we've ever made!" Moe said. "We have enough to buy wood and sateen!"

While Otto was busily hammering and sawing, Moe remained behind the store to man the spider booth. With each passing day, fewer and fewer people came to visit. Moe marked the price down to one penny. But the huge early crowds never returned.

"I suppose everyone in town has seen you by now," Moe said softly to the spider, whom she had named Orville after the famous flying Wright brother. She wondered what the spider was thinking about. Did he know that he was far from home?

Moe tracked down and smacked several of the plentiful flies in the store. She pushed the dead flies through a hole in the cardboard. The flies fell into the berry bowl, but Orville wasn't interested. She wondered if he wasn't hungry because he was homesick for the jungle, so she decorated the sides of the bowl with green leaves. That didn't help, either. Every day Orville scampered less and less around the berry bowl.

On the last morning in June, Moe came into the back of the store, where the spider's bowl was kept at night. She peered inside. "Good morning, Orville," she announced.

The spider did not stir. He did not move one hair.

Moe hurried to Otto's house and pounded on his door. "Otto! Otto, come quick!"

He followed her to the store. "Maybe he's sleeping," he said quietly, peeking from a safe distance.

"What if he's dead? Poor Orville!"

"Let's give him a few more hours to be sure. We don't really know that much about South American spiders. Maybe he's only hibernating," Otto suggested.

By noon the next day, Orville had not budged. "I think," Moe said sadly, "we need to plan a funeral. I better tell Winnie."

Winnie was the funeral expert. She had organized countless elaborate ceremonies for dead birds, gophers, goldfish, cats, and dogs. Once she had even created a magnificent funeral for an earthworm. This was her first tarantula burial.

With proper pomp, Winnie instructed Otto and her sisters to tie black armbands above their elbows. The children's parade from the store grew and grew. At the head was Moe, pulling the cart with Orville's berry bowl draped in black crepe. Even the gang from Highview came to pay their respects. They helped decorate Orville's grave with dandelions

after he was lowered inside an empty Post Toasties box into a grave in Otto's backyard. Winnie sang a sad song, and Pearl sobbed loudly. Everyone agreed it was a very fine funeral, and Moe decided that maybe the children from Highview weren't so bad after all.

Chapter 12

For the next two days, Moe and Otto hammered and sawed in Otto's backyard. The barn became their workshop. Although they tried to work secretly, it was impossible.

"Can I help?" Winnie asked. She stood in the doorway, looking wistful and anxious.

"Me, too!" Pearl said.

Otto glanced at Moe. She was struggling with the sewing machine, which had eaten a large bunch of sateen for the third time.

"I can sew," Winnie said.

"Me, too!" Pearl said.

Moe sighed. "We could use some help if we're ever going to get done on time."

"What if your sisters tell everyone?" Otto whispered. "What if they let out the secret of my design before we're finished?"

Moe glanced at the airplane. So far Otto had hammered together the body and one of the wings. The airplane looked like the skeleton of a one-winged bird. Because he never had exactly the materials on hand that he needed, he often stopped work to go search for the right piece of wood or a hammer or nails.

"Maybe my sisters can be assistants when you need something," Moe suggested. "They were pretty good at digging up all the costumes we needed for the Medicine Show."

Winnie and Pearl nodded proudly.

"But you must promise not to tell anyone what we're doing. It's a Fourth of July surprise," Otto said to Winnie and Pearl. "Can you keep this a secret?"

"Absolutely," Winnie and Pearl agreed.

The rest of the day, Winnie, who knew how to work a sewing machine, helped Moe sew together the pieces of sateen that were to cover the wings. Pearl handed Otto nails, hammers, and screwdrivers. Because she had such little hands, she easily held together the cramped tail pieces until the glue dried.

Although Otto seemed pleased that the work was

moving so swiftly, he admitted he was disappointed that their airplane funds had run out before he could buy motor parts.

"Maybe we should wait till we can afford to build a proper engine, before we do a demonstration," he told Moe. "I don't see how we can make a public unveiling yet. We're not ready."

"But tomorrow is the Fourth of July!" Moe exclaimed in exasperation. "The airplane is nearly finished. If we take it to the top of Bishop's Hill, we can glide straight into the wind. The crowd will love it. We'll be flying just like the Wright brothers at Kill Devil Hill near Kitty Hawk. They didn't have an engine on their first try. Their first airplane was a glider, remember?" Moe smiled encouragingly. Secretly she was afraid that if they waited to find all the engine parts Otto said he needed, the airplane would never be finished, and she'd never have a chance to fly.

"I suppose you're right," Otto said slowly.

"And we can always add an engine," Moe said. "That way we'll have something exciting to demonstrate *next* Fourth of July."

On the morning of the Fourth of July, Moe woke up very early. Birds sang, and faint light came from the east, beyond the grain elevator. A steady, warm breeze moved the branches of trees outside her bedroom window. Only a few clouds scudded across the sky. Perfect flying weather!

She jumped out of bed. She dressed and tiptoed down the stairs and out the back door. As fast as she could, she hurried down Main Street. Soon wagons would roll in from farms all over the county. The wagons would be filled with excited, barefoot children, mothers with sunburned faces, and fathers who would keep glancing at the sky to check the weather.

Ever since Moe could remember, every Independence Day started the same way. In the morning, the grown-ups gave long, boring, patriotic speeches outside the town hall. Then everyone went to the Old Settler's Grove, a stand of cottonwoods on the edge of town, and set up their basket lunches of cold fried chicken, corn bread, potato salad, and lemonade. Mr. Harcourt's cornet band already had a makeshift bandstand set up with lumber supplied by Critchfield's Lumber Yard. The band would play rousing songs they had practiced over and over again since Memorial Day. Next came sporting events—wrestling contests, baseball games, a horseshoe pitching contest, and a tug-of-war.

Moe walked faster. This year the grand finale would be something as original as Art Taylor—the first airplane demonstration. Everyone in Luck would gather at Bishop's Hill, waiting breathlessly while the spectacular airplane was pulled to the top. Then their faces would turn upward like flowers in a field as brave Moe McDonohugh climbed into the cockpit and waved. And then—

"Surprise, Moe!"

Otto's voice startled her so badly, she jumped. In front of the barn stood the airplane on its buggy wheels. Somehow the airplane did not look as big outdoors as it had inside the barn. Why was that? In some places the white sateen was smudged from Winnie's grubby handprints. The cockpit didn't look anything like the one in the picture of the Wright brothers' airplane. It was made from a legless rocking chair Pearl had discovered in the alley.

It wasn't perfect, Moe thought, but it was still beautiful.

"Look at this," Otto said proudly. "I hope you like the name." He pointed to the word he had painted on the sateen: *Orville.*

"It's a wonderful name," Moe whispered.

"I've been thinking," Otto said. "You know, we've never had a chance to give the airplane a test run before we present it to the public. We don't even know if it'll fly."

Moe looked at Otto in amused astonishment. Of course they hadn't tried out the airplane. They'd just finished it the night before. Moe imagined posing for the Milwaukee newspaper photograph after the historic flight. She hoped her sisters wouldn't interrupt while she was being interviewed. At last Father and Mother would be proud of her!

"Otto, how difficult can it be to fly?" Moe said. "We've spent months and months thinking about flying, reading about flying, dreaming about flying. We know more about flying than practically anyone in the county. I'm sure we'll do just fine."

"I think this morning we should give *Orville* a trial run," Otto said, "before the public demonstration."

"A trial run?" Moe asked, stunned. Was Otto serious?

"We can experiment off the shed roof. It's plenty steep, and the airplane will come down into that big pile of hay in the field." Otto cleared his throat. "Well, it doesn't hurt to be on the safe side, does it?"

"I guess not," Moe said slowly. Somehow his lack of faith sounded like a betrayal to her.

"I know what you're thinking," Otto said. "You're wondering how we'll get the heavy airplane up on top of the shed roof."

Moe bit her lip. The thought had never crossed her mind.

"Well, lucky for us, Mr. Donnelly's delivering ice early this morning. He told me yesterday he'd drive his wagon with Clem over with some stout ropes. I've got a pulley all set up so that Clem can pull one end, and the glider will rise right up to the roof on those long boards. See?" Otto pointed to two planks leaning against the shed. "Can you help me push the airplane into position?"

Moe nodded. She walked into the barn and began shoving with all her might at one end of the glider, while Otto guided the wings out the barn door.

"Hold it! Hold it!" he shouted. One of the baby buggy wheels had fallen off. After several moments, he managed to find a hammer and nails and knocked the wheel back into place.

"Ready?" she asked. Would they ever be finished in time?

"Not yet. Right wing's loose."

Moe sighed. Did Orville and Wilbur Wright ever have this much trouble getting off the ground? She waited patiently while Otto did some more hammering and adjusting. He threaded a needle and patched a tear in the wing. Just as he bit off the thread, Clem's harness bell jangled. "It's Mr. Donnelly!" Moe shouted.

"Happy Independence Day to you!" Mr. Donnelly said with a tip of his hat. In honor of the holiday, he wore a bright red, white, and blue ribbon tied around the crown of his flat straw hat. On his lapel was his shining Grand Army of the Republic pin, which he wore only on very special occasions: Independence Day and the birthday of his favorite general, Ulysses S. Grant. "A beautiful morning, isn't it? Now, what can Clem and I do for you?"

"If I attach these ropes to the back axle of your wagon," Otto asked, "do you think you and Clem can walk east so that the glider here will lift on these pulleys and be pulled up to the roof?"

"Sure thing," Mr. Donnelly replied. "Only you're certain those boards will hold?"

Otto nodded. "They're stronger than they look."

Mr. Donnelly scratched his head. He gazed at the airplane in wonderment. "So this is what you call a flying machine? It's sure a newfangled-looking contraption. Think it works?"

"Of course it works, sir," Moe replied quickly. "Otto's a genius."

Otto blushed.

"I'm glad you have such faith in him," Mr. Donnelly said, smiling. "All right, let's get to work."

After Otto attached the ropes, Mr. Donnelly said loudly, "Giddyap!" The horse bent his neck and moved forward, away from the shed. Moe held her breath. Little by little, the glider rolled up the boards toward the shed roof. Otto stood on the ground and guided the wheels up along the boards as best he could by shoving the glider with all his weight whenever it was necessary. Just as the glider almost reached the edge of the roof, one of the boards slipped. The glider teetered. It tipped. And for one terrible instant, one wing slammed against the wall. The shed shook.

"Keep pulling!" Otto shouted.

Clem strained at his traces. The glider wobbled and strained at the edge of the roof. The horse pulled. Nothing happened.

"She's stuck!" Mr. Donnelly shouted.

Otto dragged a ladder to the shed and scrambled up. While Moe held the ladder's base, Otto leaned dangerously over to one side and managed to tip the glider wing enough to dislodge it from the edge of the roof.

"Go ahead!" Otto shouted.

Clem took another step, then another. Otto climbed onto the roof and scrambled up to the flat section at the peak. Dipping down directly from this point, the roof made a swift descent toward the pile of hay on the ground below.

"All set?" Mr. Donnelly shouted.

Otto waved. He disconnected the rope from the glider and threw it on the ground. After he checked the wind direction by holding up a handkerchief, he repositioned the glider. Moe climbed up the ladder and stood beside him on the roof, the breeze tangling her hair. She waved to Mr. Donnelly and Clem below. In the distance, the first firecrackers exploded.

"Mind if I watch?" Mr. Donnelly called. "I never seen anybody fly before."

"Sure, sure," Otto said. He climbed into the cockpit.

"You think this is a good idea, Otto?" Moe bit her lip. The field below suddenly looked very far away.

"What's the matter?" Otto asked. "You scared?"

Moe gulped. She shook her head. "Nope."

"Then give me a push. Gravity will do the rest."
Otto strapped on the driving goggles that Moe had
borrowed from Father.

"You look like a daredevil pilot," Moe said.

Otto smiled rakishly. "Wait until the wind picks
up. Then, on the count of three, push with all
your might."

Moe positioned herself behind *Orville*'s right
wing. She put both hands on the wooden bar that
braced Otto's seat. Leaning over so that she could
use all the muscles in her legs and arms to push as
hard as she could, she waited for her cue.

"One . . . two . . . three . . . GO!" Otto shouted,
hunched forward as if to make himself as small as
possible.

Moe threw her weight against the airplane. The
wheels began to roll. At the edge of the incline,
Moe stopped pushing. The airplane left her hands.
It bumped and picked up speed, humming louder
and louder, faster and faster. The wings fluttered.
Orville hurled off the roof into the air.

And then, as in slow motion, the airplane tilted.
Nose-first, it careened straight down. *Crash!* In a
horrible explosion of splintered wood and tearing
fabric, the airplane smashed into the pile of hay.
Dust and dry grass flew in every direction.

"Otto!" Moe screamed. She darted down the ladder. Her legs could not move fast enough. What if he was dead? "Otto!"

Mr. Donnelly helped Moe dig through the hay and pull away wood and cloth. Where was he? Something moved under the crippled wing.

"There he is. Boy, can you hear me?" Mr. Donnelly said. He reached under the wreckage.

Moe held her breath. She thought of Orville the spider underground in the Post Toasties box, then closed her eyes and prayed.

"What happened?" Otto asked in a dazed voice.

Moe opened her eyes. There was Otto—alive! His hair was matted with dirt and spiked with pieces of hay. His face was scratched and bloody. Under each eye was a heart-shaped cut where the goggles had left a mark.

Mr. Donnelly dragged him from the wreckage to the shade beside the laboratory. "Can you move your legs? Can you move your hands and fingers?"

Otto did as he was told.

"Nothing's broke, I guess," Mr. Donnelly said. "That's good."

Otto moaned. "Look at *Orville!*"

For several moments the three of them stared at the heap of wood and fabric.

"Did I fly?" Otto asked. "I don't remember."

Mr. Donnelly shook his head. "If what you mean by flying's like a bird on wing—well, no. You fell faster than a rock in a dry well."

Otto slumped forward, his head in his hands. Moe reached down and patted his shoulder. They both knew there would be no spectacular Independence Day flight. No publicity. No shaking hands with the president. Their hours and hours of planning and work—destroyed in a matter of seconds.

Just when nothing worse seemed possible, something worse happened.

"Madeline Genevieve McDonohugh!" Flora screamed at the top of her lungs. "Where are you?"

Chapter 13

"Save us!" Moe begged Mr. Donnelly.

"Hide in the wagon," he said.

Moe helped Otto to his feet. Together they hurried to the ice truck and climbed in the back. They hid behind two enormous chunks of ice as furious Flora rounded the corner of the laboratory at full speed. Her face was red. In one hand she waved what remained of her autograph album.

"Do you know where my sister is, Mr. Donnelly?" Flora demanded, out of breath.

Mr. Donnelly stood beside the airplane wreckage, his elbows jutted out, his fists on his waist. He stared at something at his feet.

"It was sure something." He shook his head and

kicked a splintered board. "Never seen anything like it."

"Like what?" Flora demanded.

Mr. Donnelly tilted back his head and whistled. "The crash."

"Crash?" Flora studied the wreckage, too. Her brows knit together. "What crash?"

"The aer-o-plane crash. Saw everything. It went right off the roof, then *smack!*" Mr. Donnelly curved his right hand upward and slammed it into his left fist.

Flora's mouth dropped open. "My sister flew off this roof in some kind of daredevil contraption?"

"I'm not saying it *couldn't* have flown. I'm not saying it *shouldn't* have flown. I don't know about such things. I just drive my horse and wagon. I stay on the ground—"

"Mr. Donnelly," Flora interrupted, "is my sister hurt? What happened? Tell me. Tell me right this minute."

Moe peeked in wonderment through an opening in the back of the wagon. She'd never seen her sister so agitated over her health and welfare. In fact, she didn't know Flora cared whether she lived or died.

Mr. Donnelly scratched the back of his head.

"Well, Miss McDonohugh, it's like this. She's all right. But she ain't exactly here right now."

"Thank goodness!" Flora looked visibly relieved. "But where did she go?"

"Seeing how Otto wasn't doing so well, I told them to go someplace cool, out of the sun."

"Otto? That Otto boy, of course! I should have known that daredevil was involved. This was another of his fool schemes, I suppose. My sister said something about sewing sateen, but I never suspected she meant airplane wings. What has gotten into her? Not a bit of sense. Imagine, she thinks she can fly."

"Yes, ma'am. It's a crazy world we live in. Horseless carriages. Wires that talk voices. Machines that make jumpy pictures." He shook his head again. "It's a crazy world. What's that you've got there under your arm?"

"My autograph album." Flora frowned as if she just remembered what she had been so angry about only seconds earlier. "My sister ruined it."

"What'd she do?"

"Unglued private pages. See? They're all raggedy now and burnt. It was none of her business, but she took the album and she wrecked it and hid it someplace she thought I'd never find it, but I did.

It was upstairs in the attic when I went to get the flag for Father to put out on the porch pole, and that's why I'm looking for Moe, so I can make sure she gets what's coming to her—"

"Sounds serious," Mr. Donnelly interrupted, "though not as serious as broken bones. Wouldn't you say, Miss Flora?"

Flora's mouth snapped shut. For several moments she didn't say anything. "She shouldn't have taken it. The album wasn't hers. It was private."

Mr. Donnelly nodded. "You're right. Well, how do you think she should make it up to you?"

Flora's eyes narrowed. "What do you mean? An apology?" She sniffed. "A formal apology would be a good start."

"What about something else? You might as well ask for something else when you've got a person beholden to you like that. Something extra. I learned that from horse traders. 'Throw in the saddle, and I'll buy the ol' nag.' What else are you going to ask her for?"

Flora shrugged.

"I've got a suggestion," Mr. Donnelly said, and smiled. "Ask her for an aer-o-plane ride."

"An airplane ride?"

"If I were a betting man, I'd place money on it

that she and Otto rebuild this contraption. Maybe next time it really will fly."

"Why, Mr. Donnelly!" Flora laughed loudly. "And here I thought you were sensible."

"Happy Independence Day, Miss Flora," Mr. Donnelly said. He tipped his hat. "Got to be going. All my customers will be cranking ice cream makers today, and they're going to wonder what took me so long to make their deliveries." He climbed into his wagon and flicked the reins on Clem's back. The wagon jolted forward. Moe ducked. For a brief second she watched the blurred outline of her sister waving. And it suddenly seemed like an adventure to Moe—escaping this way while Flora was sent in the wrong direction. Just like the Snow Queen fairy tale in which the hounds searched for the escaped princess and never found her.

As Mr. Donnelly made his last delivery, he sang in a high, tinny voice his favorite song about his favorite subject, the War of the Rebellion:

"Where are the boys of the Old Brigade,
Who fought with us side by side?
Shoulder to shoulder and blade to blade,
They fought till they fell and died . . .
They fought till they fell and died."

As Moe listened, she thought about how happy she was that Otto was still alive. As for the airplane, well, they could always build another one, couldn't they? She took a deep breath and let out all the air at once so that she could see the vapor cloud she made in the wonderfully cool ice wagon. She closed her eyes and smelled the piney, fresh aroma of packing sawdust. "Otto," she whispered, "doesn't it remind you of Christmas in here? And outside it's the Fourth of July. Do you think it's a crazy world, like Mr. Donnelly said?"

Otto didn't answer. She could just see the whites of his eyes glint every now and again in the shadows. "Why didn't it work?" he asked finally. "That's what I can't figure. Maybe the tail was wrong. Next time—"

"Next time?"

"Of course. You didn't think we were going to give up that easily, did you?"

"No, never," Moe said. Even though he couldn't see her face in the shadows, she hoped he could tell she was smiling.

The wagon lurched into Mr. Donnelly's cavernous barn. Clem's hooves made hollow sounds on the wooden floor. The wheels rolled to a halt.

"Last stop," Mr. Donnelly bellowed. "Everybody off."

Moe and Otto tumbled out of the back of the ice wagon. Moe brushed the sawdust from her arms and legs. "Thank you, Mr. Donnelly," she said as she watched him remove Clem's harness. "You saved my life."

"Ah, now, it's up to you to make amends with your sister. And if I were you, I'd stay out of her private stuff from now on." Mr. Donnelly winked.

"Never been in this barn before," Otto said. He squinted and gazed at the old harnesses and horseshoes and barrels lining the back wall. Otto traced the rotted rim of an old-fashioned wooden wheel. "What's this from?"

"The kind of big covered wagons that came west and brought the folks that settled this area years and years ago. Called them Conestoga wagons. Nobody makes them anymore."

"And what's that up there, hanging from the ceiling?"

Mr. Donnelly looked up. "That's an old-fashioned wagon umbrella. Don't know why I keep it. Doesn't fit any wagon I own now, that's for sure."

Otto kept staring at the black umbrella that hung like a sleeping bat with its great black wings folded.

He licked his lips. He blinked hard. "If you don't need that umbrella, can we have it, sir?"

Mr. Donnelly laughed. "Why, sure. If you can get it down, it's yours. The thing's not doing me any good. Now, if you'll excuse me, I've got to give Clem his oats and be on my way. Don't want to miss the speeches."

Moe held her breath as Otto scaled the wall on the ladder. He unhooked the heavy black folded umbrella from the wall. As he stepped down the ladder rungs, she could see his arm shaking. When he finally stepped safely onto solid ground, he turned to her triumphantly.

"This is exactly what we need!"

Moe looked at him quizzically. Perhaps the crash landing had injured his brain. What could they possibly want with a dusty old wagon umbrella? Otto didn't own a horse. He didn't own a wagon. And it wasn't going to rain today. So why on earth did he think he needed a wagon umbrella?

At the base of the handle was a steel attachment that once fit in a socket on a wagon seat. Otto opened the umbrella, which was covered with dusty, heavy black waterproof fabric. It looked just like an ordinary umbrella, only much larger—nearly five feet wide.

"All the steel ribs are unbroken. No holes. And would you look at this handle? It must be at least one and one-half inches thick. Wouldn't surprise me if it's made of ash," Otto said. "It's magnificent!" He struggled to lift the umbrella and stood beneath it, grinning like a fool.

Moe sneezed from the dust. "Have you lost your mind, Otto Price? There isn't a rain cloud in the sky."

"But you said you wanted to be the first girl aeronaut in Luck, Wisconsin, on the Fourth of July. Well, this is your chance."

"What are you talking about?"

Otto collapsed the umbrella. He heaved it up onto his skinny shoulder. "If you want to find out, you'll have to follow me."

Chapter 14

Moe did not say a word as they hurried past the buckboards filled with picnickers. Young men with their hair slicked back and parted trotted by on their best horses. Everyone seemed to be in a hurry to get to the Old Settler's Grove. Moe felt like a fish swimming upstream, but she followed Otto, who carried the big umbrella over his shoulder as if it were a flag. *Crash!* A firecracker exploded. A boy with a sticky, orange-smeared face ran past with a paper filled with little firecrackers.

When they arrived at the laboratory, Otto did not pause to gaze at *Orville* on the ground, the sateen still flapping in the wind. When Otto made up his mind to start some new project, Moe knew there was no stopping him. At this moment he had that resolute look in his eye, and she knew it was best not to interrupt.

"Bring the ladder over here so we can climb up on the roof!" Otto called.

Moe dragged and lifted the ladder into place. She helped him carry the heavy umbrella onto the roof. Sweat streamed down her face. The wind had picked up and was blowing in from the east so that she could hear the sound of the cornet band playing "Stars and Stripes Forever." She didn't mind missing the concert. She knew something historic was about to happen. Right here on Otto's laboratory roof.

"Ready?" Otto said. Eagerly, he opened the umbrella. Wind gusted. Together they gripped the handle to keep the unwieldy umbrella steady. "Here's the plan. I'll hold on to the handle and take a flying leap over the edge of the roof. The umbrella will do the rest."

"You mean, you'll fly?"

"Absolutely."

"And where will you land?"

"The haystack."

"You sure you want to jump off this roof so soon again?"

Otto gave Moe an impish look. Another fire-cracker exploded.

"What I'm trying to say," Moe shouted, "is can I go first this time?"

"You really want to?"

Moe glanced at the pile of hay and the airplane wreckage below. She knew there was no certainty that the old umbrella would work. What if it fell apart in midair?

She took a deep breath. Those kinds of worries hadn't stopped Wilbur and Orville or Art Taylor, had they? This was her big chance. She bit her lip and wiped her sweaty palms on her skirt. Gripping the umbrella handle tightly, she held it up. But just as she was about to jump, she heard a voice shout, "Moe! Stop!"

She looked down. There was Flora, red-faced, waving her arms.

"What are you doing?" she demanded. "Father and Mother have been looking everywhere for you. They're frantic. Come down this instant."

"I can't," Moe called, smiling. "I'm about to be-come the first girl aeronaut in Luck, Wisconsin."

"You'll break both legs. Oh, please come down."

Flora's upturned face reminded Moe of a sun-flower. She had never seen her sister look so concerned, so anxious. It was touching, really. Maybe Flora wasn't as awful as she thought.

"Will you forgive me for stealing your autograph album?" Moe shouted. "I'm sorry, really I am."

Flora nodded emphatically. "Yes. Ben Price is a horrible, rude boy, and I hate him. Now come down."

Moe smiled. "Not yet. You see, if my flight's successful, I want you to be the *second* girl aeronaut in Luck, Wisconsin. Is that all right, Otto?"

"Sure," Otto said, and grinned.

For once Flora could not think of anything to say. She just stood there, her mouth agape.

"Ready, Moe?" Otto asked.

Moe nodded. Somewhere beyond Norman Dubie's hayfield and the fairgrounds, a series of firecrackers exploded one after the other. The speeches must have ended, because a roar went up that sounded like distant applause and cheering. Before she lost her nerve, Moe knew she must take to the sky.

She thought of Grace, the hawk's wings outstretched, soaring. Gripping the umbrella handle tightly with both hands, she stood at the roof ridge and started running. When she reached the edge, she tucked her feet under her. Solid ground—gone!

The umbrella bucked, filled with wind, and lifted her in a sunward arc. In that marvelous moment she heard Otto cheer, and she looked down at the ground and saw her sister's amazed face. At last, yes, she was flying!

About the Author

Trained as a journalist, Laurie Lawlor worked for many years as a freelance writer and editor before devoting herself full-time to the creation of children's books. She enjoys many speaking engagements at schools and libraries, and her books have been nominated for many awards. She lives in Evanston, Illinois, with her husband, son, daughter, and two large Labrador retrievers. Her books include *Addie Across the Prairie, Addie's Dakota Winter, Addie's Long Summer, George on His Own, How to Survive the Third Grade, The Worm Club,* and *Little Women* (a movie novelization). Her nonfiction work, *Shadow Catcher: The Life and Work of Edward S. Curtis,* won the Carl Sandburg Award (1995) and the Golden Kite Honor Book Award for Nonfiction (1995).

About the Illustrator

Jane Kendall has illustrated more than a dozen children's books, and is the author and illustrator of *Miranda and the Movies,* a young-adult novel about the early days of silent film. Her illustrations for *Come Away with Me* were inspired in part by family photographs dating from 1908. Ms. Kendall lives in Cos Cob, Connecticut, where she writes for *Greenwich* magazine and collects antique children's books and hats from the 1920s.

𝕴n her hometown of Luck, Wisconsin, in 1908 Madeline "Moe" McDonohugh is convinced excitement and adventure are right under her nose!

Heartland Series

Come Away with Me 53716-4/$3.99
Take to the Sky 53717-2/$3.99
Luck Follows Me (Coming mid-October 1996)

By Laurie Lawlor
Illustrated by Jane Kendall

 A MINSTREL® BOOK

Published by Pocket Books

Join Megan,
Max, Keith,
Chloe, and
Amanda as
they ride into
each new
adventure!

SHORT STIRRUP
C L U B ™

#1 BLUE RIBBON FRIENDS
54516-7/$3.99

#2 GHOST OF THISTLE RIDGE
54517-5/$3.99

#3 THE GREAT GYMKHANA GAMBLE
54518-3/$3.99

#4 WINNER'S CIRCLE
00098-5/$3.99

 A MINSTREL® BOOK

Published by Pocket Books